WOBAR

and the QUEST for the MAGIC CALUMET

Henry Homeyer (signature)

HENRY HOMEYER

Illustrations by
JOSHUA YUNGER

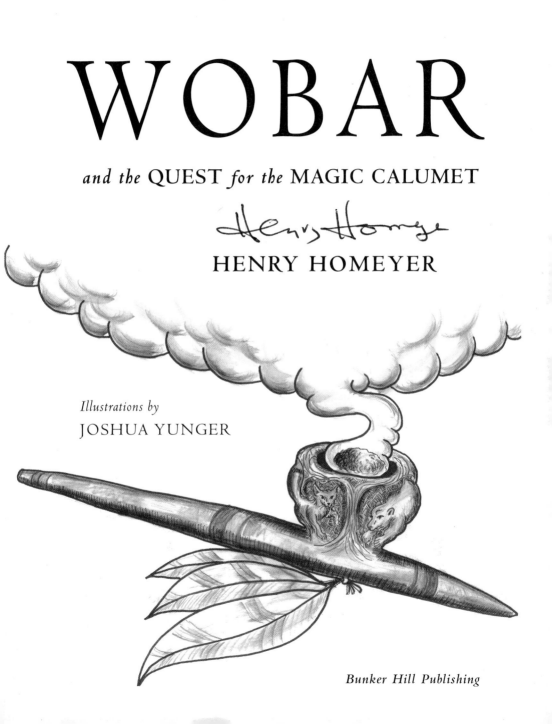

Bunker Hill Publishing

Dedication

FOR NARDI REEDER CAMPION, 1917–2007
Author, Editor, Friend

Your help in editing *Wobar* made all the difference: you made me believe in the book and helped me to continue to keep looking for the right publisher. Thanks for the refrigerator magnet with that all-important quote from Calvin Coolidge:

"Nothing in the world can take the place of Persistence. Talent will not; nothing is more common than unsuccessful men with talent. Genius will not; unrewarded genius is almost a proverb. Education will not; the world is full of educated derelicts. Persistence and determination alone are omnipotent. The slogan 'Press On' has solved and always will solve the problems of the human race."

www.bunkerhillpublishing.com
by Bunker Hill Publishing Inc.
285 River Road, Piermont
New Hampshire 03779, USA

10 9 8 7 6 5 4 3 2 1

Text Copyright ©2012 by Henry Homeyer
Illustration Copyright ©2012 by Joshua Yunger
All rights reserved.

Library of Congress Control Number: 2012937199

ISBN 9781593731083

Designed by Joe Lops
Printed in China

Contents

CHAPTER 1

Trouble at School

$\sim$

"IN TWENTY-SIX YEARS of teaching fourth grade, I've never been bitten by a student before," said Mrs. Murphy. "I'm not sure he belongs in our school."

Wobar's teacher and the principal of Woodstown Elementary School sat facing his mother. It was the first day of school, and Wobar was already in trouble. Mrs. Murphy's right hand was bandaged, and she had an angry scowl on her face.

Mr. Benson, the principal, nodded. "I've looked at his records from his other schools. He's always been a troublemaker, despite his good grades. Of course, he's only been here one day."

Wobar's mother sighed. "Yes, he's had trouble before. He's a good boy, and he means well, but kids make fun of him because of his name, and because of that mustache."

Mr. Benson cleared his throat. "This is an elementary school, so we have no official policy about mustaches, but I don't think children should be coming to school with facial hair. I'm sure the school board will agree. He'll have to cut it off."

"But you see," said Wobar's mother, "this is no ordinary mustache. And Wobar is no ordinary boy. I guess I'd better explain.

"One cold winter morning I opened the door, and there he was, a newborn baby, wrapped in a blanket. His face was red with cold, but he wasn't crying. He had a smile on his face.

"Clenched in his tiny fist was a piece of paper, with the word "Wobar" written on it. He had a full head of hair, which is not unusual, but he also had a mustache. Unlike other newborns, his hair never fell out. Neither did the mustache."

Mrs. Murphy looked at her and said, "Well, that explains it. I thought he was wearing some kind of silly glue-on mustache and told him to take it off. When he wouldn't, I tried to pull it off. It didn't come. When I reached out to try again, he bit me and drew blood."

"His mustache is very sensitive," Wobar's mother said. "We've made him shave it off, and he says he can feel the pain of each hair being cut. The few times we've insisted, it grew back bigger and bushier in just a few hours. If he had shaved it this morning, for example, it would have been even bigger by lunch."

Mr. Benson and Mrs. Murphy exchanged glances. They looked doubtful. Wobar's mother continued her story.

"We called the police, but his birth mother was never found. We started calling him Wobar because of that paper, and never changed it when we adopted him," said Wobar's mother. "Wobar is supposed to rhyme with low bar, but kids call him Woe-bear or Wob-are, and he gets mad."

Meanwhile, outside the window of Mr. Benson's office, Wobar was hiding in the shrubbery. He had run away from school that morning and had been hiding all day. It was a warm September day, and the windows were open. He could hear every word being said.

"Wobar is different than other children. At six months of age, he was walking and running around the house. At one year, he could talk. He could carry on a real conversation. And he was strong. Wobar could do things nobody else could. He was never afraid of anything or anybody. If we spanked him, he never cried. In fact, it didn't even seem to hurt.

"Wobar spends a lot of time by himself. Sometimes he goes off into the woods alone and stays all day. One time when he was just six, he was gone for three days. We had locked him in his room for doing something wrong. Well, that night he climbed out a window and ran away. We searched everywhere. The police and neighbors and friends searched the woods, but we never found him. When he came back, he said he was sorry. But he said that we should never, ever, lock him up again, or he would never come back. And we believed him.

"So you see, Wobar is different. We love him, but we can't make him be like other boys. Believe me, we've tried everything. I really worry about Wobar. He wanted so much to do well at school here. He didn't want any trouble. But now that he has gotten in trouble, I just don't know what to think. I hope he comes back home tonight."

Mr. Benson turned to Wobar's mother. "He will have to behave himself if he is to attend this school. I don't care how different he is. He will follow our rules. If he continually gets in trouble, I'll have to expel him. This state still has a reform school for perpetual trouble-makers. You need to make that very clear to him."

Wobar heard, and he understood. And he knew exactly what he had to do.

CHAPTER 2

Cougar!

෬෩

WOBAR WAS FAST. When he ran, nobody could catch him, not even his brother who was on the high school track team. So he didn't worry when he ran from the school. School had just let out, and there were plenty of people around. A teacher spotted him and shouted "Stop!" but he kept on going. He knew that once he was in the woods, they would never find him.

It was September, and the nights were already cold. The sky had clouded over, and it looked like rain. He was following a hiking trail that passed near the school and went from Maine to Georgia. He slowed down after a while, but he kept running at an easy pace. He had to cross two roads before he came to the big woods on Grantham Mountain. Each time he came to a road, he stopped and took a good look, checking carefully before dashing across. He didn't want anyone to know where he was headed.

Once Wobar had reached the big woods, he felt safe. Even though he didn't know these particular woods very well, he could get along just fine. He carried matches and knew how to build a fire to cook

on, or if he got cold. He knew the edible plants. Wobar liked living on his own in the woods.

Wobar had never told anybody, but he could talk to animals. Well, not exactly. But he could understand what they were thinking, and they could understand what he was thinking—just like they were talking. That's the way animals communicate with each other, since they can't talk the way we do. He didn't know how he was able to understand animals, he just always could, even when he was little. So he knew he would not be lonely. Animals liked Wobar.

Wobar followed a small stream until he came to a deep pool that looked like the perfect place for catching trout. Wobar loved to fish. He always kept a fishhook and some line in his backpack, even when he went to school. And he had his Swiss army knife, a big one with all the gadgets.

He used the saw blade on his knife to cut a small maple sapling for a rod and attached his line and a hook. He looked under a log and turned over a few rocks, and within a few minutes, he had several fat, juicy worms. He baited his hook and let the current pull it downstream, as it eddied around the rocks. Within an hour he had three nice trout. After cleaning them, he headed farther up the mountain to find shelter for the night.

It was nearly dark when Wobar stopped. He smelled something different. Up ahead, a tree had fallen over near some large rocks. He guessed it was hiding the mouth of a cave. He sniffed again. There was a cave and a large animal inside. He put down his fish and approached slowly. He peered into the opening of the cave.

"This is Wobar. I will do you no harm. May I enter?"

There was no response. Wobar waited. No animal came out, nor did he hear any noise. So, cautiously, he crawled in. The cave was dark, but Wobar had always been able to see quite well in the dark, even when other people said it was pitch-dark. He looked around the cave and stood up. Suddenly, with a roar, a large animal leapt up from behind a rock and knocked him to the ground.

They rolled over and over, the animal trying to bite him. It kicked, trying to scratch him. Wobar didn't want to hurt it, so he grabbed it at the back of its neck and pinched a nerve. That paralyzed the animal for a moment. He saw that it was a cougar, one of the biggest and meanest of the wild cats found in America. This one was more than three feet long, not counting the tail, and must have weighed almost as much as he did.

"I am Wobar. I will do you no harm," he repeated, but this time in the language of cats.

The cougar eyed Wobar suspiciously, and then said, "Sorry. You spoke to me first in the language of bears, who are my sworn enemies. Since you speak my language, you are welcome to my cave. My name is Roxie."

Within a couple of minutes, Roxie was able to get up and move around. She was still surprised to meet a boy who could speak her language and who knew how to fight so well. Wobar explained that he had run away from home and wished to spend a few days in the cave, or at least until he knew no one was following him.

"That'll be fine," said Roxie. "It gets a little lonely living alone. You're welcome to stay here for a few days."

Wobar went outside and broke off some small branches from pine trees to make a bed to sleep on. He was careful not to take too many from one tree, so that if a search party came, they wouldn't notice what he'd done.

When it got dark, Wobar built a fire inside the cave. It was smoky at first, but then the smoke found a way out though a crack in the ceiling. Wobar roasted the trout and shared it with Roxie. After dinner together, they sat around the campfire telling stories until late at night. When he got tired, Wobar rested his head on Roxie's chest, and she began to purr. Before long, they were both sound asleep.

CHAPTER 3

The Search Party

ROXIE, IT SEEMS, was the last cougar on Grantham Mountain. Her mate had been killed two years ago by hunters who were out looking for coyotes that were killing sheep. Her children had all gone away because they said there was nothing to do on Grantham Mountain. They had gone off to look for excitement somewhere else. Roxie had heard from a hawk that her youngest son had been caught in a steel leghold trap and was now in a zoo in the next state.

So Roxie lived all by herself in the cave on Grantham Mountain. Sometimes she considered leaving, but didn't know where else she could go. Each year, more houses and roads were built, and Grantham Mountain was one of the few places left where she could still live in peace. But sometimes she was lonely, so she was very glad to have Wobar as a guest in her cave, even if only for a few days.

Wobar liked Roxie and was comfortable living with her in the cave. He went fishing every day. One night, Roxie stole a chicken from a neighboring farm, and Wobar roasted it on the fire. Wobar collected wild blackberries and dug up the edible roots of plants and roasted them like potatoes.

Early one morning, Wobar awoke to the sounds of voices and dogs barking. A search party was approaching the cave. Roxie had warned him the day before that a hawk had reported seeing a search party not far from Grantham Mountain.

"Don't worry, Roxie," he had said. "They might look for me in barns or abandoned farmhouses, but no one would look on Grantham Mountain. Anybody knows a boy couldn't survive long on Grantham Mountain."

But he had been wrong. Soon he heard them nearby, and it was too late to run.

"Let me handle this," said Roxie. "I'll scare them off if they try to enter the cave."

"But they're probably carrying guns," said Wobar. "You could be killed!"

There was little time to think, however, as the search party quickly arrived at the cave. "Hey, Bob," someone shouted. "There's a cave up here. Wobar! Wobar! Are you in there? Come on out! It's time to go home!" A big bearded face looked in the opening of the cave. The man had a flashlight and a bloodhound on a leash.

Roxie snarled and ran toward them. The dog leapt at her, but she knocked him aside with one of her powerful paws. Suddenly, there was a deafening roar, and a shotgun blast knocked Roxie to the ground. She got up and scrambled into the cave, trying to get away. A moment later, the gun was fired into the cave. Wobar was hiding behind a big rock. Shotgun pellets bounced off the walls. He closed his eyes, lay low, and hoped for the best. The man fired three more times.

"Cougar!" the man shouted. "I've wounded it, but I don't think

I killed it. We'd better block off this cave, or it could come out and attack us."

The men rolled a huge boulder in front of the cave. The sunlight disappeared, and their voices sounded distant.

"Well, he can't be in there with a cougar, that's for sure," said one. "We better keep looking. That dog of mine sure acts like he smelled him. Maybe we'll find his bones. Cougar might have gotten him." Wobar lay still until the voices faded and the men were gone.

Roxie was bleeding badly and lay unconscious on the cave floor. Wobar needed more light to see her wounds better, so he dug a small flashlight out of his pack.

"Roxie, are you all right? Roxie, say something!" There was no answer. Wobar took off his T-shirt and cut it into strips with his Swiss army knife so he could bandage her wounds. One ear was almost torn off, and she had a huge wound on her shoulder. Wobar pressed hard on her wounds, trying to stop the bleeding. She didn't move. He bandaged the wounds and then went to open the cave.

Wobar was almost as strong as a full-grown man, but he couldn't budge the boulder that closed off the cave. The men had rolled it downhill and jammed it against a fallen tree in front of the cave. Wobar knew he had to get Roxie to a vet or she would die. But they were trapped inside, and there was no way out.

Wobar stopped to think. Their cave went deep into the mountain, and in the far back there was a river. Water ran through the cave, then disappeared underground. That river had to go somewhere, and he was pretty sure that it flowed into the trout stream. He wondered if it would be possible to escape from the cave by swimming underwater.

Wobar was a strong swimmer, and he could hold his breath for a long time. But he didn't know how far he'd have to swim underwater to get out. And it would be totally dark. He tossed a stick in the water and watched as it swirled around and disappeared. He shuddered.

He went back to see how Roxie was doing. Although the bleeding had slowed, her breathing sounded funny, and she was still unconscious. Once again, Wobar tried to move the boulder, this time using a branch to pry it loose. But it was no use. He couldn't get out. Unless the men came back soon, Roxie would surely die, and he would slowly starve to death.

CHAPTER 4

The Underground River

W OBAR STOOD BY the entrance to the cave wondering what to do. He listened for the men, willing them
to come back. If they did, he would gladly turn himself
in so he could save Roxie. He would holler and bang stones on the
boulder to get their attention. But there was no sound from outside,
no sign of the men coming back. He knew he would have to act fast
to save Roxie. He went to the back of the cave to see if he could
escape by the river.

Wobar threw another stick in the water and watched it disappear
underground. He had no choice. His only chance was to try to swim
out of the cave. He took off his sneakers and his jeans and tested the
icy water with his toes. He twirled his mustache nervously. Then he
eased into the cold water and took several deep breaths. The water
sucked at him, trying to pull him down toward the deep dark hole.
He held on to the edge for a moment, then went in, headfirst.

The water was moving so fast that Wobar didn't have to swim.
He just let the current pull him along. He kept his arms out to protect his head, fending off any rocks. He must have gone about thirty
yards when he felt the water moving faster. There was a hole in front

of him, and the water was rushing to get through it. "This is it," thought Wobar, as he felt the size of the hole. "It's too small for me, and I can't swim back. I'm going to drown."

Wobar pushed with all his might to get through the hole in the rock. No luck. He grabbed the edge and shook it. Suddenly, part of the rock broke loose, and he shot through the opening. The water slowed down, and he soon found himself floating to the surface in a huge dark underground cavern. He swam to the side, all out of breath.

After a short rest, Wobar made his way along the edge to the other side of the cave. He could hear water gurgling as it was sucked down fast. Would this river really go outside? Or would it go to an underground lake in the center of Grantham Mountain? Wobar had no choice but to keep on going. He took a deep breath and let the river pull him down and away. The cold water chilled him right to his bones.

After a little while, the river slowed down, and Wobar began to swim underwater with the current. Up ahead, he finally saw light! He swam as hard as he could, and just as he was totally out of breath, he came to the surface. He'd made it! As he'd hoped, he was in the big pool where he'd fished for trout. He swam to the side, pulled himself out, and collapsed on the bank. He was cold and tired, but still alive.

Moments later, Wobar was running back up the mountain. When he got to the cave, he knew just what to do. First, he dragged away the dead tree that was in front of the cave. Then he found a big stick and used it to pry loose the boulder that blocked the entrance. He ran inside, checked on Roxie, then quickly put on his sneakers and dry jeans. His T-shirt was ruined, so he would have to go bare-chested.

Carefully, Wobar lifted Roxie in his arms and carried her out of the cave. Although she must have weighed as much as he did, Wobar managed to lift her limp body up and onto his shoulders. He headed down the mountain, moving carefully so he wouldn't fall and hurt Roxie.

When Wobar's family first moved to Woodstown, their dog had been hit by a car. His father had brought Bobo to an animal hospital on the other side of Grantham Mountain, and the vet had been able to save his life. So that's where Wobar was headed.

Wobar was afraid that the doctor might recognize him, even though he hadn't talked to him, and Wobar's brothers and sisters had been there. Still, his mustache made him more noticeable than most kids. The vet might call his parents or the police, but Wobar had to take that chance if he wanted to save Roxie.

Roxie was very heavy, and Wobar wanted to stop and rest, but he didn't dare waste any time. He didn't want to go on the roads, so he kept in the woods and cut across fields only when he had to. Finally, he saw the animal hospital ahead, and only then did he stop.

Wobar knew he had to disguise himself. He took out his Swiss army knife and opened the scissors. Snip, snip, snip. "Ouch, that hurts," he said to himself. He cut off his whole mustache even though it hurt terribly. He knew it wouldn't be a perfect job, not without a mirror, so he rubbed a little dirt over his lip when he was done. Now he was ready.

The Veterinarian Has Suspicions

∞

WHEN WOBAR RANG the bell at the animal hospital, a friendly looking woman answered the door. "My goodness," she said. "Just look at you. You're all covered with blood! Who are you? What happened?"

"My name is Bobby Jones, and I'm new in town" he said." I was playing in the woods and I found a big animal that's been shot. I think it's a cougar. I tore up my T-shirt to help stop the bleeding. I tried to bring it here, but it's too heavy for me to move. Please have the doctor come quickly." Wobar faked a little sob.

"Why of course, I'll get the doctor at once," she said and disappeared inside. As soon as she went inside, Wobar ran to the side of the house and found where the overhead wires came in. Using his Swiss army knife, he opened a gray plastic box near the electric meter and cut a couple of very small wires. Then he raced back to the door and waited for the doctor. A moment later, the doctor and his wife came out.

"Oh please, doctor," said Wobar. "Please, come help. There's a

hurt animal in the woods over there." He pointed across the field to the woods.

"Okay, let's go!" said the doctor. All three jumped into the jeep parked out front, and the doctor drove quickly across the field to the edge of the woods. Wobar led them to Roxie and begged the doctor to do something.

"Hmm," said the doctor as he looked at Roxie. "This is pretty serious. I'm not sure I can save her. But I'll do my best." The doctor and his wife lifted Roxie into the back of the jeep, and they all climbed back in.

When they got to the animal hospital, they brought Roxie inside, and the doctor went right to work on Roxie, while his wife and Wobar waited.

"What did you say your name is, young man?" asked the doctor's wife.

"Eddie Jones," said Wobar. Then he remembered he'd said Bobby Jones the first time. "Actually, my name is Robert Edward Jones. My father is Robert Jones, so my parents call me Eddie. But at school they call me Bobby. We live in the trailer just over the hill."

The lady gave Wobar a funny look. "You must be freezing cold without a shirt on. And your hair is all wet. Let me find something warm for you to put on. You go clean up, and I'll bring you a shirt and make some cocoa."

By the time Wobar had washed off Roxie's blood and combed his hair, the cocoa was ready. He put on the shirt, which was clean and dry but much too big. Wobar drank his cocoa and ate four chocolate chip cookies. They were very good, and he was hungry. Wobar hoped the doctor's wife wouldn't ask too many questions because he didn't like to lie. He knew it was wrong to lie. It was just that he didn't want to get caught.

"So, you live in that trailer on the other side of the pond?" asked the woman. Wobar nodded his head. "Maybe I'd better call your parents and let them know you're here. It's nearly dark, and they might be worried. What's your phone number?"

"I don't know," said Wobar. "We just moved in."

"That's all right, I can call information," she said and picked up the phone. But nothing happened. Wobar had cut the telephone wires.

Just then the doctor came out. "Well, I guess our furry friend will be all right," he said. "I put in quite a few stitches and gave her a shot. She's just coming to. But I don't know what to do next. Cougars can be very mean, so I don't dare keep her here. I guess we'll have to let her go and hope for the best."

His wife gave him a look. "James," she said, "I need to talk to you." They went into the next room and closed the door.

Wobar put his ear to the keyhole. Even with his extra good sense of hearing, he could just barely hear them.

"James, something funny is going on. First this boy said his name was Bobby Jones, and then he said it was Eddie Jones. He doesn't know his own phone number, and all of a sudden our phone doesn't work. I wonder if he's really Wobar, that boy everyone's been looking for. Maybe you should go for the police. Why don't I keep him here while you drive to town?"

"You know," said the doctor, "you might be . . ."

Wobar didn't need to hear any more. It was time to run.

CHAPTER 6

The Haunted House

⌒◠⌒

WOBAR RUSHED INTO the operating room. "Roxie! Roxie!" he said. "Wake up!"

"Where am I?" she asked. Roxie lifted her head and looked around. She was dizzy and felt sick to her stomach.

"You're in the animal hospital. I think the doctor's wife figured out who I am. Can you walk? We've got to go."

"I don't know. I feel funny. Can't we wait awhile?" asked Roxie.

"The doctor is going for the police. Come on, I'll help you."

Wobar helped Roxie stand up on the table, then picked her up and put her on the floor. Roxie wobbled, then took a few steps.

"It hurts to move, but I guess I can walk. I'll give it a try. Let's go."

Wobar poked his head out the door to see if anyone was watching. The doctor and his wife were still in the next room. He motioned for Roxie to follow him, and they tiptoed out the front door.

Wobar knew that they couldn't go far, but he had to find a place where Roxie could rest undisturbed. He knew the police would be looking for them, but they couldn't go back to the cave. It was too far for Roxie to travel. Where could they hide?

Wobar thought hard as he walked through a field of tall grass. His big brother had told him about a haunted house in Woodstown. It wasn't far from the animal hospital. Although Wobar didn't believe in ghosts, he didn't like the idea of spending the night in a haunted house. But who would look there? It was the perfect place.

"Wobar, I can't walk much farther," moaned Roxie. "We have to find a place to rest."

"Okay. I know just the place. There's an abandoned house about a mile from here."

Roxie walked very slowly. Wobar kept looking around for the police.

"Wobar, I'm sorry, but I can't go any farther." Roxie stopped and lay down. Let me stay here. You run or you'll be caught. I've lived a good long life. It doesn't matter what happens to me, but you're young. You must escape." Then Roxie closed her eyes and passed out. Wobar waited to see if she would wake up, then carefully picked her up and went on.

Finally, Wobar came to the haunted house. He stopped and put Roxie down on the grass. It was a big wooden house, and some of the front windows were broken. He listened. He heard a noise that sounded something like a moan. He listened again. Nothing.

Slowly, Wobar went up the steps to the front door. The door was ajar, and he pushed it open. Then he heard the noise again. It was not like any noise he had ever heard before, sort of a low screech mixed with a moan and a cry of pain. Wobar wanted to run, but Roxie needed to rest, and what better place to hide than in a haunted house?

The house smelled like wet newspapers and mildewed furniture. There was broken glass all over the floor. Whoever had lived here must have left in a hurry, because all the furniture was still in place. There was even a newspaper on the table, but it was eight years old. Wobar brought Roxie's still limp body inside and put her on a couch near the fireplace. Then he went outside to find some firewood.

Once Wobar had built a fire, the house seemed a lot less scary. He poked around the kitchen and found some cans of corned beef. He opened one and fed some to Roxie, who had woken up and was feeling a little better. He explained how he'd gotten the doctor to save her that afternoon and why they had to run, even though he'd cut the phone wires.

They had just settled down to sleep when suddenly a cold breeze passed through the room, and Wobar could sense that someone—or something—was there.

"Who is it?" he asked. There was no answer. Then he heard the noise again. First it was in the cellar, then he heard it upstairs. It was a groan, a moan, a whisper, then a scream. Wobar wanted to run, but Roxie couldn't. She was too weak. He twirled his mustache nervously, which, in the hours since he'd cut it off, had already grown back to its original length.

"My name is Wobar. I will do you no harm. Who are you?" There was no answer. Crash! Behind him a lamp fell to the floor. He turned around quickly. No one was there. A picture fell off the wall. The front door closed itself, and with a loud click, it locked. Now there was no way out.

"My name is Wobar," he repeated. "Who are you? What do you want?"

There was a long silence. Finally, a deep voice said, "I am the ghost named Simon. You're supposed to be afraid of me, just like everybody else."

Wobar thought for a moment. "Simon," he said, "I'm not afraid of anybody, not even ghosts. We're in trouble. This is my friend Roxie, the cougar. Roxie was shot, and we need a place to stay until she can walk. Couldn't we stay here? Please? Pretty please? We'll do anything you want. You must be lonely living here all by yourself. Wouldn't you like to have some friends? Roxie and I can keep you company for a few days. We could have fun together. I love ghost stories."

The ghost was perplexed. Little boys were supposed to be afraid and run away from him. But it's true, he thought, it's pretty lonely being a ghost in a haunted house. Nobody had lived in this house for a long time.

"Well," said the ghost "we'll see. I'm not used to having company. You can stay here tonight, and I'll see if I like having friends or not. It's been a long time since I've had one."

Since Wobar was very tired, he lay down next to Roxie on the couch and soon fell sound asleep.

CHAPTER 7

Hiding from the Police

T HE NEXT MORNING, Wobar woke up early. Roxie was still asleep on the couch when he got up. He tiptoed outside and looked around. He tried to figure out what he would do if the police came looking for him. They couldn't run away, that was for sure, because Roxie was still too weak. He needed to get some good nutritious food for Roxie so she would get her strength back. And he knew that he would have to make friends with Simon the ghost if they were going to stay in the house.

Wobar climbed a tall pine tree in the yard and took a look around. He could see fields, woods, and the road that led to town. He climbed down and had just stepped inside the house, when he saw a police car coming up the road.

"Wake up, Roxie!" he shouted. "The police are coming!" Roxie looked up.

"What are we going to do?" she asked sleepily.

Wobar thought for a moment. There was no time to run away. They would have to hide somewhere in the house. "We'll hide upstairs. Come on." He ran up the stairs, with Roxie following as fast as she could manage. "Wait here," he said, as he reached the top

of the stairs. Wobar took a quick look in each of the four rooms on the second floor, but there was no good place to hide.

A second set of stairs went up to the attic, but these were closed off by a door. Wobar tried to turn the knob, but it was locked. "Uh-oh," he thought. He heard the police car come to a stop outside. Then, without warning, the door opened by itself. Wobar started up the stairs, with Roxie following.

Part way up, Roxie lost her balance and fell. She crashed against the wall and let out a small moan. Wobar turned to look and Roxie was gone! He started down the stairs. He couldn't believe she had just disappeared. She had been right behind him, and the door at the foot of the stairs was still closed.

Wobar heard car doors slam shut and two men talking. "I'll watch the outside," said one. "You go in and search the house. Look every-where: cellar, attic, inside the closets, underneath the furniture."

The policeman entered the house. "Come on out, Wobar!" he shouted. "We know you're in here." He began on the first floor. He looked in the living room and the kitchen. He checked the din-ing room and the pantry. He looked under the couch. He looked behind the drapes. He came back to the living room and saw blood on the couch.

"We're hot on their trail," he called out. "They must have been here last night." Just then there was a loud noise in the basement. "I hear something in the basement. I'm going down. You check outside to see if there's another way out of the basement and guard it if there is."

The policeman turned on his flashlight and started down the stairs. Crash! Something fell. He reached the bottom step and waited. He moved his light from side to side. He stopped. He listened. He heard nothing, not a sound.

Meanwhile, Wobar had stopped on the stairs. There still was no sign of Roxie. He leaned against the wall and suddenly the wall moved. He felt himself fall. His head hit something hard, and he was knocked out.

In the basement, the policeman started moving furniture and boxes, trying to find Wobar. It was dark and dusty. He aimed his light at an old glass vase. It shattered into little pieces. Then behind him, he heard another noise. A box fell over. He turned to look when he heard chains rattling and a low moan. But he didn't see anybody.

"Come on, Wobar," he said. "You can't scare me. I don't believe in ghosts!" But suddenly a figure appeared wrapped in an old blanket. The policeman thought it was Wobar, and he leapt at it. But when he grabbed it, there was nothing but a blanket.

"Holy cow!" he yelled. "This place really is haunted!" He ran up the stairs, through the living room, and outside. "Hey, O'Brian," he said. "Let's get out of here! I just saw a ghost!"

Officer O'Brian chuckled. "You've seen too many late night movies," he said. "Okay, you stay here, and I'll investigate. But the boys at the station are going to get a good laugh out of this one."

He went inside and down to the basement. He searched everywhere. He checked the first floor. He searched the second floor. He looked under the beds, He looked in the closets. He was starting up the stairs to the attic, when he heard a sound.

Wobar had just come to. When he'd leaned on the wall, a panel had moved, and he'd fallen into some kind of secret room. He was covered with dust, and he needed to cough. It was completely dark. He felt Roxie next to him and heard her breathing, but she didn't move. Wobar could hear the policeman on the stairs. If he, too, touched the panel, their hideout would be revealed.

The policeman stopped on the stairs to listen. He was just about to lean on the wall when out of nowhere a big wooden barrel came rolling down the stairs. It was full of dishes that were falling out and breaking all over the place. He tried to get out of the way but couldn't. He let out a loud yell just as it rolled over him.

CHAPTER 8

A Narrow Escape

O

UTSIDE, THE OTHER policeman heard his partner's shout and the sounds of breaking dishes. He pulled out his gun and went inside. "Hey, O'Brian," he yelled. "Where are you? Are you all right?" There was no answer.

"This isn't funny," he thought. "Something is going on here, and I intend to find out who is up to these tricks. If it's that Wobar kid, he's really going to be sorry."

The policeman quickly checked each room on the first floor, then on the second floor. He opened the door to the attic stairs, and with a great clattering of dishes the barrel rolled onto the floor in front of him. O'Brian opened his eyes and let out a groan.

"O'Brian! Are you all right?"

"Yeah, I guess so. But don't stand there gawking, go get him!".

With gun drawn, the policeman stepped over his partner and went up the attic steps. He was going to catch whoever had pushed the barrel of dishes down the stairs. He knew the culprit had to be there because there is only one way out of an attic. He was pretty sure Wobar was up there.

The attic was dim and dusty. He cautiously moved about, look-

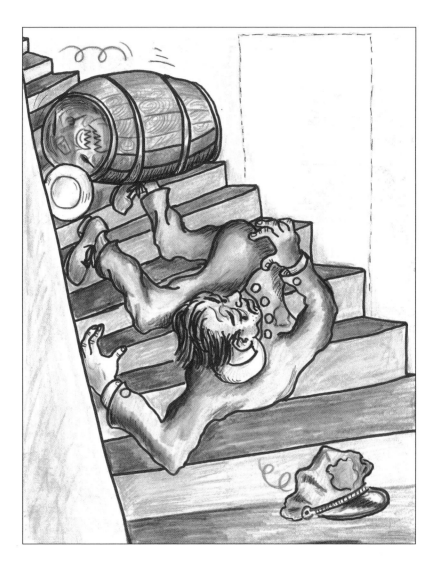

ing behind the stored furniture and big boxes. But still he found nothing. He hurried downstairs and saw that, except for some cuts and scratches, O'Brian was okay.

"This place really is haunted," O'Brian said. "There isn't anybody up there, and there's no way anybody could have gotten away. As much as I hate to admit it, only a ghost could have done it."

The two policemen went downstairs. Just as they were about to get in their squad car, they saw a man running across the field, headed for the woods.

"That must be him!" said one. "Whoever rolled the barrel down the stairs must have escaped somehow. Maybe he climbed out the window. Let's go!" They jumped in the car and started bumping across the field hoping to catch the man.

Meanwhile, Wobar and Roxie were still in the secret hiding place. Wobar was wondering how they would get out when he heard a voice.

"That was a pretty good trick, wasn't it?" It was Simon the ghost, who had suddenly appeared out of nowhere.

"What happened?" asked Wobar, rubbing his head where he'd bumped it falling into the secret room.

"Well, first of all, you should understand that there is a panel in the wall of the attic stairs, which leads into this secret hiding place. When Roxie fell, she crashed against it. It opened, and she disappeared. I'll have to admit I pushed her because there wasn't enough time to explain what to do. Then the same thing happened to you when you went back to look for her."

"What happened to the policemen?" asked Wobar.

"I tried to scare them off by breaking things and making noises.

But they kept thinking it was only you, so I had to get rough. I rolled a barrel of dishes down the stairs on Officer O'Brian."

"Uh-oh," said Wobar. "I hope he isn't hurt." Roxie let out a little noise as she sat up and looked around.

"Nothing serious," said Simon. "Anyhow, when they went outside, I turned myself into a man running across the far field. The police gave chase. They think that whoever caused all the trouble in the house was the guy they saw running away. Of course, I disappeared as soon as I got to the woods. They'll keep on looking for a long time—but they'll never find me."

Wobar breathed a sigh of relief. "But what if they come back?" he asked.

"You don't need to worry. You and Roxie can come back to this secret hiding place. Look at this. There's a latch on the inside so you can lock the room. Even if they push on the wall, nothing will happen. You and Roxie wait here for a while. When I'm sure the coast is clear, I'll let you know."

CHAPTER 9

The Magic Calumet

⟨⟩

THAT NIGHT WOBAR, Roxie, and Simon sat in the living room with a small fire in the fireplace. Wobar had closed the cloth drapes over the windows, so the light from the fire wouldn't be seen from the road.

"But why did you decide to save us?" asked Wobar.

"Well," Simon said, "it does get lonely being a ghost in a haunted house. Besides, you were in trouble. But you didn't think about yourself. You wanted to help Roxie and to make friends with me. You knew, somehow, that I was lonely. It's been a long time since I've had a friend. So I decided to save you, even though it meant hurting the policeman."

Wobar thought about that for a long time. He, too, knew what it was like to be lonely. And he did miss his family. "Simon," asked Wobar, "I don't know if you want to tell me, but why are you a ghost living all by yourself in a haunted house?"

Simon thought for a few moments and then he said, "It's okay. I'd like to tell you what happened. I've had to stay in this house for over two hundred years. Every time someone moved in, I would make noises that scared them away. It's what ghosts do. Even the nice

people got scared away. The last family left without even taking their furniture."

Roxie had fallen asleep on the couch and must have been dreaming because she began to whimper. Wobar stroked her soft, silky fur, and she went back to a peaceful sleep. Roxie would be okay. She just needed time to heal.

"You see," said Simon, "most people never turn into ghosts. They die and go to heaven to be with their friends and family. If they're lucky, they even get to be with their pets. But every now and then, something delays this. I think it's because some ghosts have unfinished business. So we have to hang around until we figure out a way to do whatever has to be done. Then we can go to heaven."

"Do you know what you have to do?" asked Wobar.

"I do, but I can't do it all by myself. I've pretty much given up hope of ever finding someone who would help me."

"If I can help you," said Wobar, "I will. Just tell me what I have to do."

"It all started a long time ago. I was a soldier in the Revolutionary War. One day, my men and I were marching through the forest when we heard voices up ahead. We knew the British were not far away, and I thought we could ambush them. I told my men to spread out in a half circle so we could capture them. I told them to listen for my signal. I would hoot like an owl if I wanted them to shoot." Simon sighed.

"The men I was leading were a rough bunch, and I'll have to admit I hadn't done much to enforce discipline. There was one man in particular that I didn't like, who was always making trouble. The men called him Bad Bert. But I needed men, so I never sent him away.

"My men began to crawl through the forest. I could hear rustling up ahead and went to investigate. Suddenly, an owl hooted, and my men began to fire into the trees! I was so stupid! I should have known better than to use an owl's hoot as a signal. We couldn't see who was there, but they were shooting anyway. I yelled for them to stop, but it was too late. It wasn't the English. They had just shot three Indians who were just passing through the forest. It was awful!"

Wobar sat on the edge of his chair. "Then what happened?"

"I cautiously approached. Only one Indian was still alive, and he held up his hands in a gesture of peace. He was clutching a beautifully engraved silver pipe. The pipe had an eagle, a bear, a fox, and an otter carved on it. He was trying to speak, so I bent over him to listen."

"'Please,' he said, 'help me. I am carrying the magic calumet of my people. It is a peace pipe. My people have been attacked many times. But by sharing this magic calumet with our enemies, we have always been able to stop wars. Its magic can stop any war, even one far away.' The Indian, who was speaking his own language, paused to see if I understood him. I had traded with the Indians and spoke several native languages. I told him to go ahead, that I understood.

"'I wish to bring it to the American general,' he said. 'The one called Washington. This calumet has more power than any other. It has been blessed with special powers to make peace, more than any other pipe. It is magic.' He coughed then put his head down."

Simon paused, then said, "I knew that both the British and Americans had been trying to get the Indians to help their side in the Revolutionary War. I couldn't imagine why this Indian would want to give the pipe to Washington. I waited. The Indian was bleeding badly, so I put pressure on his chest to slow the blood flow. After a few minutes, the Indian began to speak again.

"'I hope that my people are not pursued and attacked the way the

Iroquois were. If Washington sees that many Indians are peace loving and unwilling to fight for either side, maybe he will let my people hunt and farm and raise our children. I do not want my children to die the way I am—in a war that has nothing to do with my people.'

"I stayed by his side for over an hour, but there wasn't really anything I could do. I told him I would bring the calumet to General George Washington, but I never knew if he heard me. Finally, with a groan, he died.

"I picked up the calumet and admired it. I knew that peace pipes generally were plain stone pipes, but this one was made of silver and decorated so nicely I believed it really was very special. I showed it to my men, and then I put it into my pack. I never should have shown my men the pipe, but I did. Late that night, when everybody was asleep, I heard a noise, but I was so tired I fell back to sleep. When I got up in the morning, my pack was gone, along with the pipe and all the money to pay my men. Bad Bert was gone, too.

"We chased after him that day, but never saw him again. The war went on for years and many people were killed. If only I could have delivered the pipe, the war might have ended sooner. And the magic pipe could have prevented so many other wars, too. But it's lost, and until I find it, I must remain a ghost."

"But why do you stay here?" asked Wobar.

"A few months after I lost the pipe, my men and I were ambushed by the British. I was killed not far from this house. And although ghosts can do many things, we can't travel far. So I've had to stay near here, and I've been living in this house ever since."

By then it was very late, and Wobar was tired. "Let's go to sleep, and tomorrow we can make a plan. I'm sure we'll be able to find the magic calumet somehow."

CHAPTER 10

The Plan

T HE NEXT MORNING Roxie was feeling much better and went outside for a walk. Simon warned her to stay away from the road, so no one would see her. Wobar and Simon sat down to make plans.

"If you want me to find the magic pipe, you'll have to tell me all you know about the man who stole it," said Wobar.

"His name was Bert Blandish. He was big and tough and loved to fight. I don't really know where he went, but I heard that he headed south to New Orleans. That's a long way from here, and he left two hundred years ago. It's awfully nice of you to want to help, but I don't think there's any way you could ever find the magic pipe, not in a million years. I'm afraid I will always be a ghost."

Simon felt so sad he wanted to cry. But ghosts can't cry, so he sat there making an odd noise that sounded sort of like the hiccups.

"Don't be sad, Simon," said Wobar. "There must be a way to find the pipe. After all, it's made of silver. Something like that wouldn't just disappear. Maybe it's in a museum. As soon as Roxie is better, we'll go to New Orleans and start looking for it.

"If Bad Bert settled in New Orleans, maybe I can find his great-

great-great-great-great-grandchildren. Maybe they'll let me have it so there can be peace in the world. Or maybe they would agree to sell it. You were supposed to give the pipe to General George Washington—who later became president. If we give it to the president of the United States now, that should be just as good. And then you won't have to be a ghost any longer."

Simon knew that Wobar wasn't an ordinary boy. There was his mustache and his ability to talk to Roxie. But even so, it didn't seem possible for anyone to find the magic pipe. And Simon didn't want to get Wobar into any more trouble.

"Wobar," he said, "you shouldn't even try. You don't have any money. How can you get to New Orleans? What are you going to eat? Where will you stay? If you and Roxie travel together, surely someone will recognize you and send you back to your parents. You might even get sent to reform school!"

"Let me worry about all that" said Wobar. "The first thing I'll have to do is make good disguises for Roxie and me. Let's go to the attic and see what we can find."

So Simon and Wobar went to the attic to look for disguises. Simon pointed out a trunk of old clothes, and Wobar picked out some things for himself. He found a hat his grandfather would have liked. It was a fedora with a wide brim that he could pull down to hide his face. He found a tweed jacket, khaki pants, and some leather shoes that fit quite well.

"I've watched my mother take in my brother's clothes to fit me," he said. "I bet I can fix these things up to fit me. There must be a needle and thread around here somewhere. But I've still got to think of a disguise for Roxie. What can we do to make Roxie look like something else? "

After a little while, Roxie came inside from her walk. Wobar had picked out a dress and a bonnet for Roxie to wear.

"Wobar!" said Roxie, "You've got to be crazy! I can't wear a dress! I'm a cougar, and I run on four legs. If somebody saw an old lady in a dress running on four legs, they would be sure to stop to look—and ask questions!"

"I know," said Wobar. "But just try these things on. You'll have to learn to walk on your back legs. It's not so hard."

So Roxie put on the dress and the bonnet. The dress was long enough to cover her hind paws when she stood up. Wobar found a shawl, which he put over her shoulders so she could hide her front paws. But sadly enough, she still looked like a cougar. A cougar wearing a dress, but a cougar nonetheless.

"Don't worry, Simon" said Wobar. I'll think of something else for Roxie. In the meantime, Roxie, why don't you practice wearing the dress and walking on your back legs?"

Roxie didn't like the idea at all. But she really wanted to go with Wobar and needed a disguise. He was such a good friend, and he might need her help. Besides, now it would be too lonely to live all by herself on Grantham Mountain.

CHAPTER 11

The Disguises

⟨∿⟩

FOR ONE WEEK, Simon, Roxie, and Wobar lived together in the haunted house. A couple of times a patrol car came by to see if anybody was there. Each time, Wobar and Roxie hid in the secret room and waited quietly until the police went away.

Every day, Roxie got stronger, and at the end of the week, Wobar removed the stitches the vet had put in. Wobar slipped off into the woods and went fishing every day for food, and twice Roxie went out at night and caught rabbits. Wobar didn't like her to go out while she was still recuperating, but Roxie wouldn't listen to him. He particularly didn't like Roxie killing rabbits, because Wobar liked rabbits. He had known rabbits and could talk to them, even though they all talked baby talk and most weren't very smart.

"I'm a cougar," Roxie said. "I can't stay inside this old house all the time and have you bring me food. I've got to be able to hunt for myself. If I just sit around, I'll never get my strength back. And rabbits are delicious. Yum!"

They had time to kill while Roxie healed, so Wobar taught her to understand spoken English. She learned quickly, and when needed,

he sent her explanations in the language of cats, which his brain could send to her without making a sound.

Wobar fixed up the old clothes to make them fit. When he got dressed up, he looked sort of like a short old man. He found an eyebrow pencil and practiced drawing wrinkles on his face. In a drawer in one of the bathrooms, he found some baby powder, and he mixed it with water and worked it into his hair and mustache to make them look white.

He also knew that if he were to fool anybody, he would have to walk like an old man. So he cut himself a walking stick and spent hours walking slowly with a slight limp. He practiced talking with a deep voice so that people wouldn't guess he was really a boy.

Roxie hated wearing a dress and a frilly bonnet. She said it made her look silly. But she did get better at walking on her back legs, and by the end of the week, she could even go up and down stairs without falling. But she knew that she needed a better disguise, something that would let her be the animal she was.

Simon continued to worry. He tried to convince Wobar that he shouldn't try to find the magic pipe. He pointed out that if Wobar went back to his family, he and Roxie could come visit him often in the haunted house. Then he would have a friend, and it wouldn't be so bad being a ghost.

"But Simon, I can't go back," said Wobar. "I'm in trouble at school, and by now I'm sure they would surely send me to reform school for being a truant, and they would try to catch Roxie and put her in a zoo. You've been here for two hundred years, and nobody has ever helped you. So I'm going to! Besides, if we find the magic peace pipe, there won't be any more wars. I've *got* to do it."

Simon knew that Wobar was right. If only he could find the

magic pipe, everything would be all right. Wobar would be a hero, and nobody would be mad anymore.

One thing still bothered Simon. Although he didn't want to say so, Roxie's disguise wouldn't fool anyone. She didn't look like a little old lady, even if she dressed like one. Wobar even tried putting lipstick on Roxie, but you just can't make a cougar's face look like a lady's.

Finally, Simon had an idea. "Roxie, I've got it!" he exclaimed. "Why don't we paint you to look like a dog? There's paint in the basement, and Wobar could paint you to look like a firedog. You know, a Dalmatian. White with black spots."

Roxie thought that was an awful idea. She hated dogs and didn't want to look like one. But finally she agreed. "At least I won't have to wear that silly dress and walk on my back legs," she said.

That night, Wobar packed so they would be ready to leave early in the morning. He found a small suitcase for his clothes, and although he didn't tell Roxie, he packed her dress, too. They found the paint, but decided to wait until morning to try it on Roxie.

CHAPTER 12

Getting Started

ᚲᚲ

ARLY THE NEXT morning, Wobar and Roxie got ready. Wobar painted Roxie white with black spots. He put on a collar he'd made from an old belt. He even had a fake dog tag for her that he'd made from a tin can. Roxie looked pretty convincing, though a bit large for a Dalmatian. They thanked Simon for all his help, said good-bye, and set off down the road.

Wobar had studied geography in school so he knew it was a long way to New Orleans and that they couldn't walk there. Since they didn't have any money, he knew they couldn't fly there, or take a bus. But they might be able to take a train.

Not far from Woodstown, there's a train station with a big freight terminal. Freight trains passing through would stop for an hour or two to take on more cars or to unload freight. Wobar knew that they couldn't ride a passenger train, but he thought it might be possible to hop on a freight train.

As they walked along the road, Roxie kept listening carefully for cars. Each time one came, she warned Wobar, and they hurried into the woods to hide. Even though their disguises were pretty good, they didn't want to push their luck. Once or twice, there wasn't

anywhere to hide, but the cars went by without taking any notice, which they took as a good sign.

Once they got to town, Wobar pulled his hat down to hide his face as much as he could. He walked slowly and limped like an old man. He fiddled with his mustache whenever anyone looked his way. Roxie kept close to him and tried to act like a dog, snuffling around fire hydrants and pulling on her leash whenever she saw a cat.

Wobar knew that once they hopped on a freight train, it might be a long time before it stopped. They had to get some food to take along or they would be miserable. And Roxie needed food to build up her strength.

"Okay, Roxie," he said, "this is what we have to do. I'm going to go in a store and steal some food. I'll also grab a notebook and a pencil so I can keep track of what I've stolen. That way I can pay it back once we've found the magic pipe."

"But Wobar, how are you going to steal food without getting caught? Maybe it would be better just to go hungry."

"That's why I said we. We'll work as a team. I'll find a small grocery store that only has one person behind the counter. Once I'm inside, you'll have to make a disturbance outside. When the owner runs outside, I'll grab what we need and put it in the suitcase. It's our only chance."

Slowly, Wobar and Roxie ambled down Main Street. They went by a drugstore and a hardware shop. They passed a Laundromat and a diner. Then Wobar spied what he was looking for: Spencer's Family Market. Outside on the sidewalk was a big display of fruits and vegetables. He tied Roxie's leash to a fruit table outside and went in.

"May I help you, sir?" asked the man behind the counter.

Wobar looked down and mumbled in a deep voice, "Cookies. I'm looking for my favorite brand of cookies. I forget what they're called."

"Third aisle on the left. We're a small store, but we've got a good selection. Have a look," said the grocer.

Just then there was a terrible crash outside. Roxie had tangled her leash around the leg of the fruit table and given a strong pull. Over went the table. Apples and pears spilled. Melons rolled into the street. Peaches went every which way.

"Heavens to Betsy!" cried the grocer, racing out of the store.

Quickly, Wobar went to work. He grabbed a large jar of peanut butter, a loaf of bread, and a quart of chocolate milk for himself. He couldn't decide if Roxie would like cat food or dog food, so he took some cans of each. He stuffed the food in the suitcase. He stuck a notebook and a pen in his pocket and hurried toward the door.

Outside, fruit was everywhere. "Fido! You bad dog! Look what you've done," Wobar yelled. He helped the man pick up the table and put the fruit back.

"I'm so sorry," he said. "Fido is a nice dog, but he's not very smart. Here, let me help you with those apples. "

Wobar deliberately knocked some more apples off the table and bumped into the man as he pretended to try to catch them. Roxie jumped up and down wagging her tail.

"Forget it mister, forget it," said the storekeeper. "Just get your dog out of here and leave me alone! This is a mess, but I don't need your kind of help. I'll take care of it."

Wobar apologized again, but the man said something rude under his breath. "Get out of here. Just to go away!" he grumped. They left and headed toward the railroad yards. Wobar felt terrible about stealing the food. He knew he would come back to pay for the things he had taken. He just didn't know when.

CHAPTER 13

Sneaking Around

WOBAR AND ROXIE knew they couldn't ask anyone where to find a freight train heading south. Somehow they would have to sneak into the freight yards and just figure out what to do. Of course, if they got on the wrong train, they might end up in Mexico City or Montreal or Kalamazoo, Michigan. Wobar didn't think that trains went to Timbuktu, but that was a possibility, too. In fact, Wobar wasn't at all sure that hopping a freight train was a good idea. But he didn't say that to Roxie. He didn't want her to worry.

As they approached the train yards, Wobar walked slower and slower. He looked for a way to get in, but there was a high wooden fence everywhere to keep people out. Suddenly, Roxie came up with an idea.

"Wobar, I've got it! If you stand on your suitcase, you should just be able to reach the top of the fence and pull yourself up and over. Then I'll grab the suitcase in my mouth, get a good running start, and jump over. Once we're inside, we'll figure out what to do. "

Sure enough, Roxie was right. Wobar could just reach the top. He pulled himself up, looked around to be sure no one was watch-

ing, and climbed over. A moment later, Roxie came sailing over the top, suitcase in mouth.

"I'll bet you didn't know I could jump like that, did you, Wobar?"

"No, I didn't. But that trick might come in handy later. Quick! We'd better hide. Here comes somebody."

Wobar and Roxie dove into the tall grass and lay still. A man drove by in a pickup truck and parked not far away. He got out and started their way. Wobar held his breath and tried not to move, even though the grass was tickling his nose. The man walked past the freight cars, stopping from time to time to write something on his clipboard. Suddenly, a voice boomed out from nowhere.

"Hey, ribber snapper fornswaggle. Chegitout."

Or at least that's what it sounded like. Wobar couldn't figure out what was going on, or who was talking. Someone was on a loudspeaker, giving directions. The man got back into the pickup and drove away. But Wobar still didn't dare to move. They would just have to wait and see what was going on before they made a move. The ground was wet, and Wobar was getting chilly.

"You wait here," said Roxie. "I'll check this place out. We can't sit here all day, you'll catch cold." So Roxie trotted off to explore the freight yards. After a while, she came back.

"I didn't learn anything about where the trains are going or when," she said, "but I found a safe place to hide. There's an old shack that isn't being used. We can hide there and stay out of sight. Keep low and follow me, Wobar."

By crawling on his hands and knees, Wobar stayed low enough that the tall grass hid him from view. When they finally reached the shack, Wobar was tired and cold. His hands and knees hurt from crawling over sharp stones. He lay down to rest on a piece of a cardboard box inside the shack. He was just about to fall asleep when he heard a gruff voice.

"Didn't nobody ever teach you no manners?"

Blocking the doorway was a man with a stick in one hand and a bundle in the other. He was dirty, his clothes were all patched, and one of his front teeth was missing. He glared down at Wobar and gave a kick at Roxie who had fallen asleep by the door.

"This is my place, and I don't recollect inviting you in," said the man.

Wobar didn't know what to do, and there was no way to escape. So he took a deep breath and using his gruffest, meanest voice said, "Watch it mister, that dog of mine is trained to kill. One false move, and it's all over. You may not like people coming in your shack, but I don't like people kicking my dog. And I don't think she likes it either."

The man stepped back and took a good look at Roxie who was now wide awake. She let out a deep growl, showing her huge teeth.

"No need to get ugly. You surprised me, that's all. Why don't we all sit down and get comfortable. It's going to be awhile before any freight trains leave here. And why don't you tell your dog to stop looking at me like that?"

CHAPTER 14

Oscar the Hobo

∽

"MY NAME IS Oscar," said the man. "I'm a hobo, and I've been riding freight trains for a long time. I've just been visiting my sister up in Woodstown, like I do every year. I've been using this shack for a good many years, and it's like a second home to me. So I was surprised to find another hobo here. Not many of us hoboes riding freight trains anymore."

Oscar seemed nice enough, but Wobar didn't think he should use his real name. After all, if Oscar had just come from Woodstown, he might have heard about a runaway boy named Wobar. Besides, he knew he should get used to pretending he *wasn't* Wobar.

"My name is Pete," said Wobar. "And this is my dog, Spot. We always travel together. She keeps me company. Where ya headed?"

"It's gettin' too cold up here," said Oscar. "I'm heading south. No particular place. Maybe I'll go to Florida. Try to find some work and a place to sleep. Maybe I'll go pick oranges. Where you going?"

"We're going south, too. Thought I might go to New Orleans.

Never been there, but I hear it's a nice place. Say, you wouldn't happen to know when the next train south is leaving, would you?"

Wobar and Roxie were in luck. Oscar said that by late afternoon a train would be leaving for New York, and he would be taking it. They could all travel together. Wobar was relieved to know which train to take. And once he reached New York, he should be safe. Nobody would be looking for him there.

While they were waiting for the train, Oscar built a small fire and cooked up a tasty stew. He even gave some to Roxie, who had been glaring at him ever since he had given her that kick.

"You say your sister lives in Woodstown?" Wobar asked, between bites of stew. As usual, his mustache got messy when he ate. One side always turned up, while the other turned down and got into his food. "I don't suppose there's much excitement in a place like Woodstown."

"Oh, it's nice enough. But I always get bored after a few days. Why, the only exciting thing that happened there in a long time has to do with some kid. Gobar . . . or Wobar . . . something like that. Got in trouble at school and ran away. Everybody was talking about it. Seems he tamed a mountain lion and has been living in the hills with it. People think he comes out at night and steals food and chickens, that sort of thing.

"Tricked an animal doctor into sewing up the cat after it got shot, then ran off without paying the bill. They think he cut their telephone wires. Seems there's a five-hundred-dollar reward for anybody who catches him. And the school is mad 'cause he bit his teacher, and he's been playing hooky for weeks now. Like I say, it's a small town with not much to do. That kid is all anybody's been talking about."

Wobar choked on a bite of stew. "Holy Toledo!" he thought. "This is worse than I'd imagined. We better get outta here, and fast." He wasn't sure how good their disguises were, or how convincing he was. And he noticed that Oscar kept looking at Roxie. He knew that five hundred dollars would be a big help to someone like Oscar.

"That sure is a funny looking dog you got there," asked Oscar. "What kind is it exactly?"

"Well, she's actually a mixed breed. Mother was a firedog and her father was a lion hunter. Special breed from Africa for hunting lions. They're really big and can even climb trees. That's where she gets those special claws. They're for climbing trees," said Wobar.

"And that hair sure looks funny. Almost looks like somebody painted her," said Oscar. He peered suspiciously at Roxie.

"Oh, that's nothing" said Wobar. "She had a lot of fleas, so I had to wash her in some special stuff. It hasn't come off yet."

Just then they heard a train whistle, and a freight engine backed up to hook on to a line of cars.

"That's us!"said Oscar. "Train 10-56 gettin' ready to head south. Follow me! Let's go!"

CHAPTER 15

Catching the 10-56

&

THE 10-56 MOVED slowly through the freight yards heading south. There were boxcars full of lumber, bricks, ball bearings, and cheese. Empty tank cars and coal cars going back to be filled up again. Oscar led the way, running with his bundle and his stick. Wobar and Roxie were a few steps behind, trying to keep pace with the train as it began to speed up. Across the freight yard, someone hollered, and a pickup truck headed their way.

"That's our only chance," yelled Oscar. He pointed to an open boxcar just ahead. As he came abreast of the car, he tossed in his stick and the bundle. With one quick move, he vaulted up and into the moving boxcar. Next, with an easy bound, Roxie was through the open door. She stood in the open doorway with Oscar and looked at Wobar, who was having a hard time keeping up.

"Come on, Pete! You can make it," shouted Oscar. Wobar ran faster, but the train was picking up speed. With a burst of energy, he reached the open door and tossed in the suitcase. He was just about to leap up, when he tripped.

Down he went on the gravel of the track, skinning his hands and tearing the knees of his pants. As he looked up, he saw the last open

car moving away with Roxie and Oscar. Looking back, he saw the pickup truck coming his way, bouncing fast over the rough dirt road. He knew that he had but a moment or two to make his escape.

Quickly, Wobar jumped to his feet. He ignored the pain and began to run as fast as he could. The last car, the caboose, was just up ahead. The train whistled as it left the yard, but it didn't slow down. The pickup truck was blowing its horn wildly. With a burst of speed, Wobar reached the caboose, grabbed the iron rail by the steps, and pulled himself up.

Meanwhile, the car with Oscar and Roxie had disappeared around a bend. Roxie didn't know that Wobar had managed to climb up onto the train. She picked up the suitcase and was about to leap from the moving train when Oscar grabbed her by the collar. He grabbed the suitcase from her and spoke harshly.

"Hold on dog, you can't jump out! You'll get killed. Stick with me. I'm not such a bad guy. Didn't I give you some of my stew?"

Roxie wasn't afraid. Wobar was her best friend, and she thought he needed help. She let out a deep growl, scaring Oscar, who stepped back. She paused for just a second, then leapt out of the moving train.

When Roxie hit the ground, she rolled twice and landed on her feet. She was in pain but that didn't slow her down. She headed back toward the freight yards to find Wobar.

"Roxie! Roxie!" yelled Wobar from the steps of the caboose as he went by. She looked up in surprise. Wobar was on the train, but by now, the train was going almost full speed. She turned and sprinted down the tracks.

"Come on, Roxie, you can do it!" yelled Wobar.

Now cougars are fast, and Roxie was used to running long distances when she went hunting. For a mile or more, Roxie kept pace with the train. Sometimes she'd get farther behind, then each time when it seemed that all was lost, she gained a little.

Unfortunately, freight trains never get tired, but eventually cougars do. Wobar was worried. He thought about jumping off, but the train was going too fast. If only the train would slow down a little bit.

Up ahead, Roxie saw a long hill. Maybe the train would slow down as it went up. If it didn't, it was good-bye Wobar, perhaps forever.

CHAPTER 16

Riding the Rails

L ATER THAT NIGHT, Oscar, Roxie, and Wobar were eating dinner in an empty boxcar bumping along the tracks toward New York City. They talked about the events of the afternoon while Wobar worked on his third peanut butter and jelly sandwich. Roxie had finished a can of cat food and was eating a can of dog food, even though it wasn't very tasty.

"You two were awfully lucky, you know," said Oscar. "I was sure one or the other of you two was gonna get left behind. Or killed. I tried to keep your dog from jumpin', but she gave me that growl again, and well, I didn't feel much like arguin' with her. She sure is one big dog. And when she growls, she shows those teeth of hers. They ain't like any teeth I ever seen on a dog before."

"She wouldn't be here but for that long hill about a mile from the station," said Wobar. "That hill slowed the train just enough for her to catch up. I was on the back platform of the caboose, urging her on. She just made it.

"After she was rested, Spot and I climbed up a ladder onto the roof of the caboose. We walked along those metal walkways on the

top of the cars until we came to this car. But I'll have to admit, I was pretty nervous each time I jumped from car to car."

"It's tricky business," said Oscar. "Me? I never go up top no more. One false step, and you're under the train. And it's lucky you made it here before that tunnel. You would have been swept right off the top and killed for sure. I sure was glad to see you. Surprised, too, when you jumped back in this car when we stopped to let the passenger train go by."

"Well," said Wobar, "we had to get inside the car where it's not so cold and windy. And our food was in the suitcase. Thanks for taking it away from Roxie before she jumped."

"That yard bull, the cop in the pickup truck?" said Oscar. "He saw us, you know. If you hadn't gotten on, he would have had you. Those guys don't mess around. They carry guns and ain't afraid to use 'em. If you didn't stop, he would have shot you in the leg. Then, when you got out of the hospital, you'd have gotten a month in jail. Maybe more. Don't know what they'd have done with your dog, never seen a dog ridin' freight trains before. Probably put her in the dog pound and had her put to sleep if nobody came for her while you were in the clink. Yup, you sure were lucky. Both of you."

"Do you think there will be any trouble when we get to New York?" asked Wobar. "I've never been there before."

"Depends what time this train gets in. If we're lucky, we'll get in at night. During the daytime, the yards are full of people. Police too. It can be pretty tricky."

Wobar was not at all pleased with the prospect of riding freight trains to New Orleans. If it was as dangerous as his first experience, he knew that he wanted to find a different way to get there.

"Oscar, you know I'm from California and don't know this part of the country very well. I thought maybe you could give me a few tips about how to get a train to New Orleans."

"*A* train? You can't get there on just one train. You'll need to catch at least six before you get to New Orleans," said Oscar. "From New York, the cars go on a barge to Jersey City. Catch another to Philly, change trains, go to Cumberland, Maryland, probably have to wait all day. You gotta change there, and the yard bulls are tough customers. But if you're lucky, you'll get the overnight train all the way to East St. Louis, getting in the next afternoon. From there . . ."

But Wobar had stopped listening. He had heard enough. He was going to find another way to get to New Orleans. He wasn't going to risk getting chased, shot at, arrested, or run over by a train to get there. He didn't know what he was going to do, but he knew he'd find another way.

CHAPTER 17

Walking the Streets of New York

T HE TRAIN ROLLED into the West Side freight terminal late the next afternoon. Trouble started as soon as they arrived. No sooner had they jumped down than they were being chased again. "Oh no," thought Wobar. "It seems like I've been running or hiding ever since I left home!"

"Hey, you! Stop right where you are!" yelled the yard bull. "Stop or I'll shoot!"

Oscar was already running zigzag across the freight yard, and Roxie was following him. Wobar was afraid, but he didn't have much choice, so he started running, too. He just hoped that the fellow wouldn't really shoot.

Two bullets went whizzing by. Wobar ran as fast as he could and quickly caught up with Oscar and Roxie. They had just gotten around the corner of a building, and Oscar was gasping for breath.

"We'd better get out of here quick!" said Oscar. "Follow me!"

Dashing and dodging, hiding behind train cars and buildings, they

made their way across the freight yards. Once they had to jump into a dumpster to hide. It smelled awful.

"P.U.! This place stinks," said Roxie. "If this is what cities are like, let's get out of here fast".

"We'll be out of here soon. And don't worry, I've got a plan," said Wobar.

Oscar decided that he would try to get a train that very night going toward Florida. "You sure you don't want to come along? It gets easier after this," he said. "And Florida is a real nice place. There's oranges just falling off the trees and great beaches, too, if you like to swim."

But Wobar said no, he'd ridden enough freight trains. He'd find another way. So they said good-bye, and Oscar pointed the way out of the freight yard. A few minutes later, Wobar and Roxie were walking along the sidewalks of New York.

Wobar noticed that all the dogs in New York were on leashes, so he put Roxie's on, even though she didn't like it. He figured it was probably a law in New York, and he didn't want any more trouble. He'd had enough already.

"Wow!" said Roxie as they ambled down Fifth Avenue. "I can't believe these buildings! They're so tall. They're even taller than Grantham Mountain!"

Wobar tried not to stare too much. They looked funny enough, and he didn't want to attract attention. But he couldn't help but peek up from under the brim of his hat from time to time. There were people everywhere. Big people, little people. People of all colors. People wearing every kind of clothing. They even saw dogs wearing coats! This wasn't at all like Woodstown. And Wobar didn't have the faintest idea where to go or what to do.

It was nighttime and getting cold. They walked downtown, while Wobar tried to come up with a plan. Although he had assured Roxie he had a plan, he only knew they had to make some money to eat and get a ticket to New Orleans. He knew he didn't want to spend the night on the street. They walked past restaurants, and the wonderful smells made them even hungrier. He looked at the long lines of people waiting to get in.

They had been walking a long time, and Wobar was tired. It's almost impossible to sleep on a moving freight train. He hadn't had a good night's sleep since they had left the haunted house. And Wobar was hungry. Up ahead he saw a little park with some benches, so they decided to stop and rest. Wobar opened a can of cat food for Roxie and made himself another peanut butter sandwich with the last of his bread.

"This cat food is awful," said Roxie. "Didn't they have any flavored like rabbits? I sure would enjoy a nice fat rabbit tonight. You said this is supposed to taste like seafood? It doesn't taste like any fish I've ever eaten." Roxie wrinkled her nose and made a face.

"I have to admit that peanut butter sandwiches lose some of their appeal if that's all you have to eat. But don't worry. We're going to earn some money tonight. Then we can buy anything we want to eat. You just wait and see. I've got a really great idea!"

Wobar really did have a plan, finally. He knew how they could make money. Enough money for food and maybe even a hotel room.

CHAPTER 18

Making Money

W OBAR'S PLAN WAS simple and seemed foolproof. He had figured out how they could make money, lots of money. Since he and Roxie could communicate silently, they would do magic tricks. It wouldn't really be magic, of course, but it would seem like magic to the people who watched.

"First we need to find an audience," said Wobar. "Then I'll tell people that my dog can talk to me, and for one dollar, I'll prove it. I'm sure somebody will want to test us. I'll put on a blindfold and cover my ears. Then they whisper a secret into your ear—something that I couldn't possibly know. You come over and pretend to whisper it in my ear, and then I tell everyone their secret. And we win the dollar!

"As soon as other people see it, they'll think there's a trick, so they'll want to try to figure out how we did it. We can offer a double-your-money guarantee: 'If Spot, the talking dog, can't tell your secret, you get TWO dollars back.' Everybody will want to try!"

"But where do we get an audience?" asked Roxie. "I've seen people going into the movies and theaters and nightclubs. But we can't go in there. For one thing, we're dirty and smell like garbage."

"You'll see, follow me," said Wobar. He got up and started walking. After a while they came to a part of town that had lots of restaurants. Outside one, there was a long line of people waiting to get inside.

"Here we are," said Wobar. "An audience. They must be bored waiting to get inside. And if they've got money to spend on a fancy restaurant, they'll probably have a dollar to prove that dogs can't talk."

Wobar and Roxie stood on the sidewalk next to the line of people. Wobar took a deep breath and shouted out, "Ladies and gentlemen, tonight you are in for a treat! For your entertainment while you wait for dinner, I would like to present Spot the talking dog!"

Most people kept on talking and didn't pay attention. Roxie was getting nervous. Wobar twirled one side of his mustache, trying to make it curl up.

"Now many of you may think you've known a smart dog or two in your day. Well, Spot is the smartest dog in the world! Not only can she understand everything you say, she can talk to me."

Roxie liked Wobar's speech. It was much better than what Wobar told the store man when she knocked over the fruit. She liked Wobar's plan.

"I realize that many of you might not think Spot can really talk. You might think this is a trick. Well, for one dollar I will prove it! That's right, folks. For one dollar I will prove it! And should Spot fail to perform, not only will I refund your dollar, I'll pay you a dollar!"

Roxie was a little nervous now. Wobar didn't have two dollars. Wobar had taught her to understand English, but she still missed some words. What if she got stage fright and couldn't tell him the secret? Then they'd be in trouble.

"Who will be the first to test Spot the talking dog? Just one dollar!"

Oh, Harold," said a woman to her husband, "This will be fun. Give the man a dollar."

"But this has got to be a trick. The guy can probably read lips or something. This is silly," the man said.

Wobar was anticipating this. "To prove that there are no tricks involved I will cover my eyes and ears." He pulled out his handkerchief and tied it over his eyes. "Now, tell Spot a secret that no one else could possibly know. I'll cover my ears."

The man gave Wobar a dollar. His wife bent down and whispered in Roxie's ear. Roxie came over and nudged Wobar, who bent down and pretended to listen while Roxie sent him a mental message.

"Her husband snores," said Roxie.

"Ladies and gentlemen! Spot has told me this lady's secret." He turned to the lady. "Is it all right if I tell your secret to everybody here?"

The lady giggled. "Well, since dogs can't talk, give it a try," she said.

"Ladies and gentlemen, this lady's secret is that her husband snores!"

People in line howled. They laughed and giggled and guffawed. But many still didn't think it was real.

"It was probably a setup," said one.

"It must be a trick," said another.

"Since some of you don't believe that Spot can really talk," said Wobar, "I will now convince you! I will blindfold myself and face away. Take out a dollar bill for Spot to see. She'll come get it. Then whisper your middle name in her ear, and she'll tell me. If anybody doubts that Spot can talk to me, show them your driver's license."

Wobar turned away and waited. A young man with long hair held out a bill. Roxie trotted over and got it.

"Melvin," she told Wobar.

"The man's middle name is Melvin!" shouted Wobar. "Am I right?"

The man scratched his head and looked surprised, but nodded. Yes, his middle name was Melvin. Still, nobody wanted to believe that Spot the talking dog was for real. All up and down the line, people kept pulling out dollar bills to test her. And every time Roxie was right. She had a hard time with the name Sebastian, but Wobar still got it. Roxie and Wobar had discovered a gold mine!

CHAPTER 19

Almost Getting
a Hotel Room

ᖰᖷ

WOBAR AND ROXIE had, indeed, struck it rich. By midnight, they had performed in front of six restaurants and a theater. They had collected, in total, 134 one-dollar bills. They were tired and hungry, but no longer worried.

"Wow," said Wobar as they headed down the street. "A few weeks doing this, and we can buy the silver pipe! I've never had so much money in my whole life! Let's go get something good to eat. I'm tired of peanut butter!"

So Wobar and Roxie found an all-night deli and ordered up more food than they could eat. Three pounds of fresh raw chicken liver for Roxie. A roast beef sandwich with potato salad and coleslaw and a quart of grape soda for Wobar. And a quart of vanilla ice cream to share between them. Roxie was ready to start on her dinner right there on the sidewalk in front of the deli.

"Not yet, Roxie," said Wobar. "Let's find ourselves a cheap hotel room. Then we can relax and eat our food without worrying about

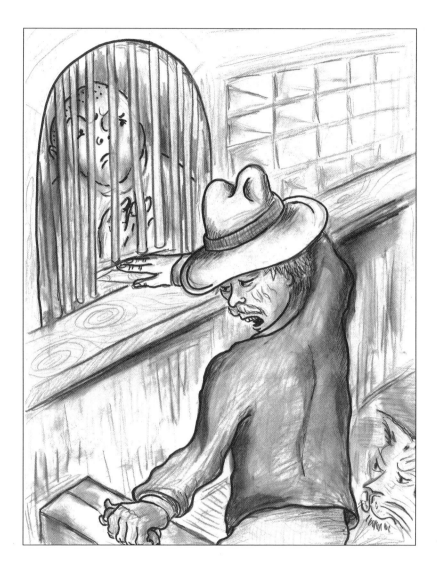

getting in trouble. For all we know, there might be a law against feeding dogs on the sidewalks of New York City. Come on, let's go before the ice cream melts!"

Wobar and Roxie were in the right part of town to find a cheap hotel. Although the first two had "No Vacancy" signs lit up, the third one flashed its neon sign: ROOMS—ROOMS—ROOMS. Wobar and Roxie walked up to the front desk. Wobar could barely see over the front counter.

"Hello!" he called. "Anybody here?"

A sleepy looking man looked out of a small office behind the counter. "Yeah? Waddya want?" he said gruffly. The man didn't seem like he was very interested in customers.

"I'd like a room for the night, please. "

"Thirty-five dollars. Cash. See the sign? No checks, no credit cards. With state and local tax that comes to thirty-eight dollars and forty-four cents. Gotta be out of the room by noon." He peered at Wobar. "How old are you, anyhow? Is that mustache real?"

Wobar ignored the question. He counted out thirty-nine one-dollar bills and paid the man, who tossed him a key.

"Up two flights of stairs, turn left. Number 206. If you need anything, it can wait till morning."

Wobar didn't like the man and didn't understand why he was so rude, but wasn't in a mood to argue. They headed across the lobby and were almost to the stairs when he heard the man hollering.

"All right, wise guy, where do you think you're goin'?"

Wobar stopped. What could he have done wrong?

"Come on, joker, you know that you can't bring a dog into a hotel in New York City! You want I should lose my license? Get that animal, whatever it is, outta here right now before I call the cops!"

"But sir, I didn't know that, "said Wobar. "Spot is a very well mannered dog and won't cause any trouble. Just let us stay tonight, please? We've come a long way, and we're very tired."

"Out! You heard me! If that thing ain't outta here by the time I count ten, you're gonna be in big trouble."

"But what about the money I paid?"

"One, two, three . . ."

Roxie gave a growl.

"Six, seven, eight . . ."

Wobar tugged on the leash, and they ran for the front door and down the steps. Their bag of groceries split open and everything fell on the sidewalk. The quart of grape soda smashed. Wobar felt like crying. Roxie was mad. She wanted to go back and scare some manners into the man. But they didn't. They picked up their things, put everything into the suitcase, and started down the street, tired and discouraged.

CHAPTER 20

The Fire Escape

◔◕

WOBAR AND ROXIE couldn't find a nice place to eat their dinner, so they just sat on the front steps of an apartment building. Wobar got out the food, and they ate until they were stuffed. The ice cream was soupy, but Roxie didn't care. Cats, even big ones like Roxie, love cream, even if it's really melted ice cream.

Roxie turned to Wobar after she finished eating. "Vanilla is great, Wobar," she said. "Does ice cream come in all flavors?"

"Well, practically all flavors. Some places even have bubble gum ice cream, and once I had peanut butter and jelly ice cream," said Wobar.

"Great! "she said. "Next time it's my turn to pick. I'm going to get rabbit ice cream!" Wobar wanted to laugh, but he was just too tired.

They had been in predicaments before, and every time they'd found a way to solve their problem. But this time they were at a loss. They didn't know anything about cities, and they didn't know what to do next. So they just got up and started walking.

After a while, Wobar stopped. "We've got to find a place to

sleep, Roxie," he said. "I don't think I can walk any farther." He put down his suitcase and sat on it.

"You get a room for the night, Wobar," said Roxie. "I'll take care of myself. Then tomorrow we'll figure something out, okay?"

"No. We're in this together. We're a team. Besides, every dog I've seen here is on a leash. It must be the law. On your own, you'd be caught and sent to the dog pound. "

"Are you kidding?" said Roxie "I'm a cougar, not a dog. I can run thirty miles an hour and jump over an eight-foot fence, even with a suitcase in my mouth, remember? Nobody can catch me." Roxie stopped talking and stared at a hotel across the street. "Do you see what I see?"

"Yes. It's a hotel, but . . ."

"No, Wobar. That ladder. There are ladders coming down the side of the hotel."

Wobar looked. Sure enough, there were metal platforms outside each window and ladders going from floor to floor. "That must be the fire escape, Roxie," said Wobar. "I've read about them. That way people can get out of the hotel in case of fire."

"Great. I'll wait outside while you go get a room. Then when you get to the room, open the window and signal me. I'll have to jump up to the first platform, but after that I can climb up the ladders, and you can let me in the window!"

Wobar went in, asked for a room, and paid for it. Once he was in the room, he opened the window and waved to Roxie. Even though she was tired, Roxie managed to leap to the first platform, and then climbed up the ladders to the fifth floor. She wasn't afraid of heights and was a good tree climber, but she avoided looking down. It was a long way to the sidewalk.

"This isn't the cleanest room I've ever seen," said Wobar, "but it will do. I'm so tired I could sleep for a week."

Wobar took a shower and scrubbed off all the dirt and grime from riding in a boxcar and hiding in a dumpster.

"Roxie," he said, "you don't smell very good. Why don't I give you a bath? I'll put on a fresh coat of paint in the morning?"

Roxie didn't like the idea of a bath. Cats never do. But she didn't like smelling like garbage either. And the paint was itchy and some of it had rubbed off and her disguise wasn't looking very good.

"We'll do better making money tomorrow if you don't stink," said Wobar. "And I'm not going to let you sleep on my bed if you smell like garbage."

So finally Roxie agreed, and Wobar gave her a bath. It wasn't nearly as bad as Roxie had thought it would be. In fact, she almost admitted to enjoying it. Wobar needed two towels to get her thick fur dry.

It was very late by then, so they climbed into bed. They were tired but happy. They weren't being chased anymore, and they would soon have enough money to get to New Orleans. The last thing Wobar heard as he drifted off to sleep was Roxie's loud purring. It was a lullaby to his ears.

CHAPTER 21

The Hotel Fire

FOR THE NEXT few days, everything went just right for Wobar and Roxie. Early each morning, Roxie would climb out the window onto the fire escape. Once Wobar got outside, he checked to be sure no one was watching, signaled Roxie, and she climbed down. They spent their days walking around New York, looking at everything.

They walked across the Brooklyn Bridge and looked at the tugboats pushing barges up the East River. They visited the United Nations Plaza, and Wobar wondered if the silver pipe could really bring peace to the world. He hoped so, but he felt a little discouraged thinking how far they still had left to go. Once they even rode the subway late at night when there was no one to keep Roxie out. They rode in the front car, watching the dark tunnel ahead. It was kind of spooky.

Roxie was most fascinated by the Central Park Zoo. She couldn't believe there were so many kinds of other animals in the world. Monkeys and seals, penguins and parrots. Dogs weren't supposed to go inside the buildings, but Wobar snuck her in anyway. She was amazed that he could talk to them all, even animals that she couldn't

understand. But she hated that the lions had to live in cages like that. They were too much like her.

"Wobar," she demanded, "do those poor lions have to live like that forever? Couldn't we help them escape?"

"We'd better not. That would get us in trouble for sure," he said. "Anyhow, lions couldn't survive in New York City. They would starve to death if we let them out."

Roxie felt sorry for the animals in cages. She told Wobar that if she ever got put in a zoo, she would refuse to eat until they let her out—or she starved to death. Wobar assured her that she had nothing to worry about. They would never get caught, so she shouldn't worry. Even so, some nights Roxie had bad dreams, and Wobar woke her up when she whimpered in her sleep.

Every evening, Wobar and Roxie stood outside restaurants and movie theaters and did their trick. And every night, they made money. Some nights they made more than other nights. Everything in New York was very expensive, but they were still saving lots of money for their trip to New Orleans, and that's what counted.

Late one night they were both sound asleep when Roxie woke up. "Wobar," she said, "Wake up! I smell smoke. I think there's a fire."

Wobar woke up. He sniffed the air. Roxie was right! The hotel was on fire! Wobar ran to the door. When he touched the doorknob, it was hot. He was afraid to open it. There must be a fire in the hallway, he thought. Quickly, Wobar packed their suitcase. He got the money from under the mattress and stuffed it in the suitcase.

"Let's get out of here!" shouted Wobar. He opened the window and climbed out onto the fire escape. Roxie followed him down the ladders to the last platform, which was about ten feet above the sidewalk. Wobar saw that there was an emergency ladder, so he pushed it down to the ground, then dropped the suitcase to the street. He was about to climb down when he stopped to think. What about the other people in the hotel? If they were asleep, some of them might die.

"Roxie! Go down the street to the corner. There's a fire alarm there. It's a red box on a pole. Pull the handle. That will call the fire department. I'm going to wake up the other people. They've got to be warned!"

Wobar had given Roxie another bath that night and hadn't painted her, so she had no disguise. She was clearly a cougar, sleek and beautiful with a long tail that lashed from side to side in her excitement. But if they were going to save the others, there was no time to worry about that. Roxie jumped down easily and ran to call the fire department.

Wobar started up the fire escape. At each room, he banged on the window. "Fire, fire!" he yelled. "GET OUT QUICK!"

People woke up and quickly climbed down the fire escape. Smoke was pouring out of some of the windows. When he reached the top floor, only one room appeared to be occupied, but nobody answered his knock. He could see a man lying in the bed. The fire engines still hadn't come.

"Wake up! Wake up!" he yelled, banging on the window. There was no answer. He tried to open the window, but it was locked. Smoke was filling the room.

Wobar didn't hesitate. He gave a quick punch with the side of his fist, breaking the glass. Then he unlocked the latch, pushed up the window, and climbed inside. He knew he didn't have time to waste if he wanted to save the man and get out alive, too.

CHAPTER 22

Sheets and a Square Knot

COUGHING AND CHOKING, Wobar made his way across the room to the bed. An old man was lying there, motionless. Wobar shouted at him, hoping he would wake up. He grabbed him and gave him a shake. But the smoke had already made him limp and unresponsive. Wobar would have to carry him out. Flames were climbing the wall by the door.

The old man was still breathing, but he was out cold, which made him hard to move. Wobar grabbed him under the arms and dragged him to the window. He draped him on the windowsill with his head outside. Fire was in the room, and a lightbulb exploded. Wobar grabbed the man by the waist and tried to push him out the window onto the fire escape. Just then Roxie arrived.

"Here, let me help." Roxie grabbed onto the man's pajamas with her teeth. She pulled, while Wobar pushed, and they got him out onto the fire escape. But somehow they had to get the limp body down six stories on iron ladders. Flames were shooting out of some of the windows below. They didn't have much time.

"What can we do?" asked Wobar. "I can't carry him down the ladder by myself. "

"Quick. Go grab the sheets off the bed," said Roxie. "Tie one around his chest just under his arms, and we'll use the other like a rope to lower him down. I'll grab the sheet with my teeth and lower him down to you. You guide him as I lower him, then we'll do it again, floor by floor, until we reach the ground."

Wobar took a deep breath and dashed back into the room. He got the sheets and sprinted back to the window. Quickly, he fitted one around the old man's chest. He tied the second to it, using a square knot, which he had learned in the Boy Scouts. He knew it would hold.

They pulled him to the edge of the fire escape with his feet hanging down. Roxie crouched a good six feet from the edge of the ladder, gripping the sheet in her teeth. As she crawled toward the ladder, the unconscious man was lowered down, dangling from the sheet. Wobar stood on the ladder below, guiding him. He eased the old man onto the platform. Luckily, he didn't weigh very much.

Wobar and Roxie worked fast to get the man down. They had to be careful because a false move could send them crashing to the street below. On each floor, they had to begin again, getting the man into place by the ladder, Roxie lowering him down, Wobar guiding him. The third floor was the hardest. Flames and smoke were billowing out of the window nearby. Some of the fur on Roxie's tail was scorched by flames as she lowered the man down. But she never faltered. They would save the old man.

Finally, Wobar reached the ground. By then, a huge crowd was watching them. Someone with a camera took their picture as Roxie lowered the man to the ground. Just then, the police and fire engines arrived, and an ambulance screeched to a stop next to them. A fireman scooped up the old man in his arms and ran toward the ambulance.

"Come on, Roxie," said Wobar "Let's find our suitcase and get out of here. You don't have your disguise on, and anybody can tell you're a cougar. I don't want to have to answer any questions about who we are."

Just then a TV truck pulled up. A reporter jumped out and went to the fire captain, who pointed at Wobar. Suddenly, there were bright lights shining on Wobar, and a reporter was shouting questions. "Who are you? Where's the animal that helped you? Are you circus performers?"

Wobar decided not to answer but to run. Roxie was nowhere to be seen, but she sent Wobar a silent message. "This way, I'm hiding down the alley to your left. Behind the dumpster."

Grabbing the suitcase, Wobar ran. He ran as if his life depended on it. He ran as if Simon's life depended on it. The reporters were no match for him. They were left in the dust.

CHAPTER 23

The Millionaire

⟨◌⟩

W OBAR AND ROXIE spent the rest of the night on a bench in a park near their hotel. Wobar pulled out Roxie's other disguise, the dress and bonnet. Roxie was surprised to learn that he had brought them along.

"I thought we agreed that I should be painted like a dog," said Roxie. "I don't think I'm very convincing as an old lady."

"It's true, but I left the paint in the hotel. And since you had a bath last night, you are clearly a cougar, *not* a dog. Someone might try to capture you and put you in a zoo. We can't take a chance."

Wobar helped Roxie put on the dress and bonnet. Wobar arranged the shawl around her shoulders, and the two of them soon fell sound asleep. They just looked like two homeless people sleeping on a bench.

The next morning, Wobar and Roxie went into a deli to buy food for breakfast. As Wobar was paying, Roxie nudged him.

"I think you'd better buy today's newspaper," she signaled silently. Wobar looked at a stack of papers and saw their picture on the front page. He took one, paid for it, and they hurried out.

Wobar and Roxie returned to the park and sat down to read the

paper. Wobar stared at their picture on the front page. "Millionaire Saved by Boy and Mountain Lion" it said in large letters. The story went on to say that C. Clement Longsworth, one of America's richest men, had been saved from sure death in a hotel fire the night before. Wobar began to read aloud.

"Mr. Longsworth had returned to visit the hotel where he had begun his career as a hotel owner over fifty years ago, only to be overcome by smoke in a four-alarm fire. Although witnesses disagree on what happened, all agree that a boy with a mustache and a trained animal saved Mr. Longsworth. The boy and the animal lowered Mr. Longsworth down the fire escape despite great danger.

"Some claim it was a leopard, others a lion, but most agreed that it was a cougar or mountain lion. Immediately after saving Mr. Longsworth, the boy and the animal disappeared and have not been seen since.

"Mr. Longsworth, who is in good condition in Beth Israel Hospital, has stated that he would like to offer a large reward to the boy and his pet who saved him."

"No way!" said Wobar. "We're famous. The only thing is, we don't *want* to be famous! That story must be appearing in newspapers all over the country. And that TV reporter might have gotten footage, too. But if we go to collect the reward, I'll get sent back to Woodstown, and we won't be able to find the magic pipe. And you might be put in a zoo."

"Maybe we should take a chance," said Roxie. "Since we saved Mr. Longsworth, nobody will be mad at you."

"Maybe. But my parents wouldn't let me go to New Orleans. Even if I don't get sent to reform school, I'll have to go back to school in Woodstown. Simon will remain a ghost because we won't find the silver pipe. And our chance to help the world find peace would be over."

"I suppose you're right. But what can we do? With our picture in the paper, we'll be recognized. And the story must be on TV, too," said Roxie.

"There's only one thing to do," said Wobar "Let's leave right now. We'll get a bus to New Orleans. Nobody will be expecting us there. And you don't look very much like a cougar in your dress. We have plenty of money. Let's go!"

CHAPTER 24

Dead Giveaway

∽

S O WOBAR AND Roxie set off to find the bus station. Roxie was out of practice walking on her back legs, and a couple of times she had to grab on to Wobar to keep from losing her balance. But after a while, she got used to it. Wobar kept pulling Roxie's bonnet down so people wouldn't notice her face.

"When you do that, Wobar, I can't see a thing," complained Roxie.

"I know, but people can't see you, either. Right now that's more important, I think. We don't want to be recognized."

When they arrived at the bus station, Wobar told Roxie to sit down and watch the suitcase while he went to buy tickets. She was glad to have a rest after walking so far on her back legs.

"Hello," said Wobar to the ticket seller. "Could you please tell me when the next bus leaves for New Orleans?"

"Sorry, buddy, the bus just left. There won't be another until 11:45 tonight," said the man.

"Oh dear. We're really in a hurry. Isn't there another way to get there?"

"I suppose you could take a bus to St. Louis, then get another one to New Orleans from there."

So Wobar bought two tickets to St. Louis. It was only a few minutes before the bus was to leave, and Wobar hurried off to buy some hot dogs. He remembered *not* to get mustard or onions for Roxie. She liked her hot dogs plain. While they were eating, some people stopped and stared.

"Look at that, Mommy," said a little boy. "That lady has claws instead of fingers. And look at those teeth." His little sister started to scream.

"That's not a lady," said their mother. "It must be some kind of wild animal wearing a dress. We'd better report this. You can't bring wild animals into the bus station. The nerve of some people!" The family hurried away and headed toward the information desk.

Wobar and Roxie got up quickly and went outside, hoping their bus would be ready to let them on. They were in luck. The bus was there, and they got right on. They brought their suitcase on with them because it had all their money in it, and they didn't dare put it under the bus with the others.

They sat near the back, and Roxie pretended to fall asleep with her bonnet pulled over her face. When the bus finally left, they were both very relieved.

The bus stopped from time to time to take on passengers and to let people eat. Wobar really wished he could get off and run around to stretch his legs, but he decided they shouldn't push their luck. They stayed on the bus all the time.

It was nice watching the scenery change as they traveled west. As they went through West Virginia, the hills reminded them of

Woodstown and Grantham Mountain. They both felt a little bit homesick for the first time in days.

"It sure would be nice to spend a few days hunting rabbits in those hills," said Roxie, gazing out the window. "I wonder if we'll ever get back to Grantham Mountain."

"I wonder about that myself," admitted Wobar. "We're a long way from home and not even halfway to New Orleans. I wish I could see my family. I do miss them, but I think we're doing the right thing. After all, if we find the calumet, we not only help Simon the ghost, it should also help to stop wars and bring peace."

The bus continued on all day and into the night. Wobar and Roxie drifted off to sleep and only awoke when the bus finally stopped in St. Louis.

"Everybody off!" called the driver. "St. Louis, end of the line."

Still half asleep, Wobar grabbed his suitcase, and they got off.

CHAPTER 25

"Borrowing" a Boat

WOBAR AND ROXIE were tired, hungry, and impatient to get off the bus by the time they arrived in St. Louis. Wobar was standing in line to buy tickets for New Orleans when he noticed his name on the front page of a newspaper. He bought one and headed out of the bus station.

"Where are we going, Wobar?"

"I don't know. But I just saw my name in the paper. I think we'd better see what it says before we do anything."

So Wobar and Roxie hurried out of the bus station and down the street. After a couple of blocks, they stopped under a streetlight, and Wobar began to read the paper.

"Hero of New York Hotel Fire Identified as Wobar," it said in large letters. Wobar quickly read the article. It explained that the hero of the fire had been positively identified as Wobar, a runaway boy wanted by police and school authorities in Woodstown. More importantly, it mentioned that a woman in New York City had reported seeing a large animal wearing a dress and bonnet in the bus station that morning. Police and bus personnel throughout the country had been alerted. It went on to say that anyone who sighted

a boy with a mustache and accompanied by a cougar should notify local police immediately."

"Holy bunny busters!" said Roxie. "What do we do now?"

"I don't know, Roxie. But we can't go anywhere by bus. And your disguise isn't any good, not if they're looking for a cougar in a dress. We're in real trouble now. I don't know how we'll ever get to New Orleans. Sometimes it seems like it doesn't pay to help people. If we had just run from the fire, we never would have been identified."

"But we had to, "said Roxie. "Otherwise, some people would have died. And certainly the old man would have died. Don't worry Wobar, we'll think of something."

But Wobar was very discouraged. It seemed like their troubles would never end. They set off down the street looking for a place to hide and wondering what to do.

After a while, they came to the banks of a huge river. Wobar and Roxie stood by it. Even late at night, tugboats were pulling barges downstream.

"Roxie, I've got it!" he said. "That's got to be the Mississippi River. We studied about it in school. It goes all the way to New Orleans, so maybe we can go by boat. See those barges carrying coal? They're headed south, toward New Orleans. Maybe we can get on one."

"I don't know, Wobar," Roxie said. We're still a long way from New Orleans. How would we ever get on one of those barges? They're moving slowly, but I'm not much of a swimmer. And our suitcase would sink, even if we could swim to one. I don't see any tied up on the banks of the river."

Wobar thought a boat of some kind was their only option. They walked along the banks of the river hunting for a boat they could take to New Orleans or at least out to a barge. Roxie had taken off the dress and bonnet and was happy to run on all four legs again.

There was a full moon, and it was almost as bright as day by the river. Finally, they came to a marina with lots of boats. Big ones and little ones. This was their chance.

"We may have to borrow someone's boat," said Wobar.

"*Borrow?*" asked Roxie. "You better not. If you get caught taking someone's boat, they won't believe you only wanted to 'borrow' it. They'd arrest you for stealing it. Then you'd go to reform school for sure, and we'd never get the silver pipe."

But Wobar convinced Roxie that it was their only chance. He knew it was wrong to steal a boat, but he would return it after they found the magic pipe. He really would, somehow. He would write it down in his notebook, just to remind himself.

"You hide in the weeds by that tree," said Wobar "I'll go down to the dock and look for a boat that isn't locked up. If anyone comes, send me a silent signal, and I'll jump in the river and hide under the dock. As soon as I find a boat, I'll whistle, and you come."

Wobar strolled down the dock. Each boat he looked at was locked up. It didn't seem like he had a chance. Just when he was about to give up, he saw a little motorboat near the end of the dock. It was tied with an old rope, and it wasn't locked up. He climbed in and tried to start the motor. He whistled for Roxie.

Each time he pulled the cord on the outboard, it almost started. But not quite. Roxie arrived and was about to jump into the boat.

"Wait a minute," Wobar said. "I can't get it started." Just then Roxie looked up. Two men were running down the dock, hollering. Wobar pulled again, but the motor still wouldn't start. They were in real trouble now.

CHAPTER 26

Gunfire!

"WOBAR!" SAID ROXIE. "We'd better get out of here." The men were fast approaching. Roxie didn't know how to swim very well, so she only had one choice. She ran right toward them, growling. She thought they would run, but they didn't. They stopped, and one pulled out a gun.

Bam! A bullet whizzed by Roxie's head. She turned and leapt off the dock. She quickly sank in the cold water. She swallowed some water on the way down, but pushed off the river bottom and came up, coughing and spluttering. If Wobar didn't save her, she knew she was a goner. She kicked her legs and tried to keep her head up. The current was pulling her downstream fast, and she couldn't see Wobar.

Wobar had heard Roxie's warning, but kept on trying to start the boat. Just as the men arrived, it started! He cut the rope to the dock with his pocketknife and pulled away from the dock. "Stop, thief!" a man cried.

Bam! A bullet sailed past the boat and splashed into the water. Wobar kept going. Bam! Another bullet, but this one hit the boat.

Wobar crouched low in the boat and headed downstream. If only he could get out of range, he would be safe. But where was Roxie?

Bam! Bam! Another bullet hit the boat, and water gushed in. Wobar could tell that in a few minutes the boat would sink.

Bam! This time the bullet wasn't even close. And that was the sixth bullet. Wobar figured the man would have to reload, so he was safe unless the other man had a gun, too. He would have to take that chance because he had heard Roxie jump into the water. And he knew she couldn't swim very far.

Wobar turned the boat and headed back toward the shore. He heard the men hollering, but there were no more shots, not for the moment. He studied the surface of the water watching for Roxie. There was no sign of her. Not a splash, not a bubble. She couldn't have drowned. Not so quickly. He wouldn't believe that Roxie might already be dead. Had she been shot?

"No, no!" he thought. "It isn't possible! Roxie can't be dead! I won't believe it! No way!"

Just then Wobar saw something. It looked like a paw hanging onto a buoy out in the river. He heard a splash. He gunned the motor and headed downstream toward it.

When Wobar arrived at the channel marker, he let out a big sigh of relief. He had arrived in time to save Roxie. The current had pulled her downstream, and she had just been able to get her claws into the rope holding the buoy. She was very cold and had swallowed a lot of water. In another minute or two, she might have drowned. Wobar stopped the boat next to her. He reached down, grabbed her, and pulled her up into the boat. He was careful not to tip over the boat.

"Are you all right?"

Roxie had swallowed so much water she could barely think. She lay in the bottom of the boat and groaned. She threw up her dinner and a lot of river water in the bottom of the boat, but she was very glad to be alive.

Wobar knew that this boat would never get them to New Orleans or even onto a barge. It was rapidly filling up with water. He stuffed his big red handkerchief in one of the bullet holes, which helped, but it didn't stop the leak. They would have to go to shore fast, before the boat sank.

Soon the police would be looking for them up and down the riverbank. The Mississippi River must be a mile wide, Wobar thought. The leaking skiff would never make it to the other side. They would have to take their chances on shore nearby or risk drowning. He pointed the boat toward shore, crossed his fingers, and hoped for the best.

CHAPTER 27

The Wooden Crate

᠀

WOBAR TURNED OFF the engine of the boat and let the boat glide up to the bank, but it made quite a thunk when it hit the shore. Wobar and Roxie climbed out and scrambled up the bank. The suitcase had gotten wet and was heavier than before.

"Hurry, Roxie. We've got to find a place to hide before the police get here." He heard a siren in the distance.

They were in a neighborhood of factories and warehouses. They ran down the street looking for a place to hide. The sun was just coming up. But everywhere they looked, there were high fences to keep people out. Some even had guard dogs that barked as they ran by. Finally, they came to an empty lot. It was full of old cars, broken bottles, and empty packing crates.

"This is the best we're going to find," said Wobar. "We can hide in that big wooden box until the coast is clear. "

They crawled inside the packing crate to wait. It was crowded inside, but at least they were out of sight. Wobar brought the suitcase inside, too, for fear somebody would see it and investigate. Moments later, a police car cruised by.

"That was a close call," said Roxie. "Another minute on the

street, and we would have been caught. But we're still in a fix. How in the world can we ever get away from here and get to New Orleans?"

"Hmm . . ." wondered Wobar "We can't take a bus. We can't take a boat. I won't try a train again. I guess . . . I guess that means we have to go by plane. "

"But how could we?" asked Roxie. "Someone is sure to spot us. And we probably don't have enough money anyway."

"I don't know. I hadn't thought about all that, " said Wobar, "But still, there must be a way to get on a plane. It's our only chance."

Wobar racked his brains trying to figure out how they could disguise themselves to get on a plane. Finally, he said, "I've got it! This packing crate gives me an idea. We'll hide inside this crate and have it sent by airfreight to New Orleans. When we get there, we'll jump out and run away!"

Wobar realized that his plan wouldn't be easy to carry out. "As soon as stores open, I'll have to buy some supplies," he said. "We'll need a hammer, nails, and a saw to fix up this crate. And a pair of hinges so we can fix a door to get out, some screws, a screwdriver, and a latch. Then paint and a little brush to put an address in New Orleans. I suppose we'd better get some food, too. I don't know how long we'll be trapped inside."

"Don't forget to buy some paint for me," said Roxie, "I'll need a disguise once we get to New Orleans."

At eight o'clock that morning, Wobar left Roxie hiding in the box and hurried into town to find a hardware store. He kept his hat pulled down and hoped that no one would recognize him from the newspaper photo. In some ways he wished he could get rid of his mustache—he was afraid it would give him away. But it hurt so much when he'd had to cut it off before. Even with scissors, he felt every hair being cut. It was almost as if he were cutting off his fingers. And besides, he wouldn't feel like Wobar without his mustache.

Nobody seemed to take any notice of Wobar when he went into the hardware store. He quickly found everything he needed, paid for it, and left. After a stop at a grocery store for food, he headed back to his hiding place. Roxie was there, waiting anxiously.

"Did you get everything?" she asked.

"Yes. And I'm glad you reminded me about your paint. Let's get you in disguise again."

Quickly, Wobar painted Roxie to look like a Dalmatian dog. Then they waited inside the crate for the rest of the day. Wobar didn't dare begin working on their crate until after dark because someone might see him and call the police.

Even though it was cramped inside the crate, they were able to get some sleep. The events of the last twenty-four hours had left them very tired. After Wobar awoke in the late afternoon, he spent his time trying to figure out how he would get the crate on a plane to New Orleans. It wouldn't be easy.

CHAPTER 28

Acme Air Freight

$\backsim$

I T WAS ALMOST five o'clock when Wobar left the crate and walked down the street to find a telephone. He went to three phone booths before he found one that worked and had a phone book. He thumbed through the yellow pages, found what he wanted, put in a quarter, and dialed.

"Acme Air Freight," said a gruff voice at the other end.

"Hello, my name is Bob Johnson," said Wobar, trying to make his voice sound grown-up. "I've got a furniture factory down on River Street. I have a crate I need sent airfreight to New Orleans right away."

"I'm afraid it's too late to do anything today," said the clerk at Acme Air Freight," but we could pick it up first thing in the morning. Where are you located?"

"My factory is at 59 River Street," said Wobar. "Tomorrow is Saturday, and the factory will be closed. I could leave it on the sidewalk out front."

"It's your risk, buddy. Somebody might steal it during the night. But if you want, we'll pick it up first thing tomorrow morning. You say you're at 59 River Street?"

"That's right. Johnson Furniture Factory. I want it rushed to New Orleans. It must arrive tomorrow. They'll pay the freight charges down there."

"Right-o. We'll take care of it. It'll be there tomorrow afternoon. Nice doing business with you. Bye."

Wobar hung up and hurried back to tell Roxie the good news. "It worked! They'll pick up the crate first thing tomorrow morning. I'd better get right to work."

Wobar found some boards in the empty lot to fix up the crate. He cut them to size with his new saw. He knew it would have to be solid so it wouldn't break open during the trip. One whole side of the crate was missing, but he soon had it repaired. He put hinges on the inside where nobody could see them and attached a latch inside to keep it closed. When he was done, it looked like a regular packing crate. It would be almost impossible to see the hidden door.

"What are you going to do about an address?" asked Roxie. "Don't you need to send it to someone down there? Someone who will pick it up and pay for the shipping?"

"I suppose so. But I'll just put a fake address on it. If Johnson Furniture Factory is on River Street here, I'll address it to Johnson Furniture Factory on River Street there. We'll just give it a different street number. Once we arrive at the airport in New Orleans, we'll climb out and run away before anybody discovers our trick."

Wobar used a small paintbrush and carefully lettered an address on the side. Johnson Furniture Factory, 237 River Street, New Orleans. Then he painted Fragile, Do Not Drop, Handle With Care, and This Side Up. The last was the most important. He didn't want to be upside down all the way to New Orleans. That wouldn't be fun at all.

During the night, Wobar dozed off from time to time, but he was too excited to really sleep. If all went well, they'd finally be in New Orleans the next day. Then he could try to find the magic pipe. Maybe their adventure would soon be over. He wished he could look in a crystal ball to see the future. Would they find the magic pipe? Would he and Roxie ever get back to Woodstown? Would he be forgiven for running away if he found the pipe? He dozed off dreaming of his family.

Just before dawn, Roxie gave him a nudge. "We'd better get ready," she said. "We should get this crate onto the sidewalk before it gets light."

With Roxie pushing and Wobar pulling, they managed to get the crate across the vacant lot and onto the sidewalk. They put it in front of Johnson Furniture Factory and climbed inside to wait. Wobar closed the door and turned the latch.

They waited. The sun came up. They waited. Three hours passed, and still no one came. Wobar worried. What if the people from Acme Air Freight didn't come? And if they did come, what would happen on the plane? Would he and Roxie freeze in the cargo hold of the plane? Would there be enough air? He knew that dogs were often shipped by plane, so he thought they should be all right.

Just as Wobar was about to change his mind about flying to New Orleans, he heard a truck pull up.

"Okay, Max, this must be it. One crate from Johnson Furniture Factory for shipment to New Orleans. Let's get it on the truck."

There was no choice. Wobar and Roxie were on their way to New Orleans.

CHAPTER 29

Landed at Last

W OBAR AND ROXIE bounced around inside their crate as the truck lurched and bumped down River Street and toward the airport. Wobar banged his head against the crate several times. Roxie felt sick to her stomach, but she didn't throw up. Finally the truck came to a stop. They had arrived at the airport.

Wobar couldn't see much, but he tried to watch what was going on through the crack he'd left between two boards. Their crate was unloaded by a forklift truck and left on a platform. They waited for a couple of hours, but nothing happened. He and Roxie ate three packages of Twinkies and waited some more. Wobar's mother didn't let him eat junk food, but this was different. They needed a quick snack to hold off their hunger.

"What happens if they don't send us to New Orleans today, Wobar?" asked Roxie.

"They *have* to send this crate today," he said. "They promised." Tomorrow was Sunday. They couldn't stay in the crate until Monday—they didn't have enough food and water. He doubted that

Acme Air Freight worked on Sundays. So they would just have to hope that something happened today.

"Maybe I should get out and see what's going on," he said.

"No, please don't go," Said Roxie. "With my luck, they'd probably take the crate as soon as you left. Then I'd be sent to New Orleans by myself. And I couldn't operate the latch on the crate myself. Claws don't work like fingers, you know."

So Roxie and Wobar waited some more. Just when they were about to give up hope, they heard someone coming.

"That's the one. Hurry up. It's supposed to go on Gulf Airways flight 603. Take off in thirty minutes," said a voice. With a jolt, their crate was lifted up and put on a cart. Moments later, they were moving up a ramp and into the belly of the plane.

The trip to New Orleans was truly horrible. They must have flown through a thunderstorm because the plane bounced up and down violently. It was cold and dark. Roxie got airsick and threw up. Fortunately, Wobar thought to bring a barf bag for her, as he knew she got sick easily. Wobar didn't feel very good, either, especially after Roxie threw up. It seemed like forever, but finally they landed. They were in New Orleans!

The crate was unloaded and sent to the freight terminal. It was nighttime, and Wobar hoped that everybody would go home soon. Then they could escape. But he heard people talking and forklift trucks buzzing around, so they had to wait. Wobar really wanted to get out and stretch his legs.

Finally, everything went quiet. Wobar undid the latch and carefully opened the door. The wood scraped against the floor with a scratching noise that sounded very loud to him. The lights were turned off. He looked around. No one was in sight. Wobar crept out and stood up.

"Come on, Roxie," he whispered. "Let's get out of here."

Roxie didn't need a second invitation. She was as glad as Wobar to get out of their little jail. They snuck around the darkened warehouse looking for a way out. They came to a big sliding door. Wobar listened but heard nothing on the other side, so he pushed on the door, trying to slide it. Nothing happened. He put all his weight on it. No go. It was locked.

"I'm afraid we're locked inside until Monday," said Wobar.

"Wait a minute," whispered Roxie. "I smell fresh air. There must be a window open somewhere."

Roxie followed her nose, and sure enough, there was a window open. Wobar pushed a crate over to it and climbed up. He peeked out. Nobody was in sight. The window was pretty high off the ground, but there was a grassy lawn below. They waited a few minutes, then he dropped the suitcase out.

Roxie jumped first and landed safely. Wobar hesitated. He sat on the windowsill. What if he broke his leg jumping down? But he didn't really have a choice. He jumped.

"Ow!" he said out loud, in spite of himself. He had twisted his ankle when he landed, and it really hurt. But they couldn't waste time. He stood up.

"Let's get away from the airport and into town. We're in New Orleans! Gimme five!" Roxie put out a paw, and Wobar slapped it. They were almost at the end of their quest. Or so they thought.

CHAPTER 30

The Fortune-Teller

W OBAR AND ROXIE didn't dare take a bus into town, so they walked. They arrived late at night, and Wobar's feet ached. Roxie was disguised as a Dalmatian and pulled on her leash like a dog. They walked around looking for a cheap hotel with a fire escape. Up Basin Street, down Bourbon Street. They heard music playing, and the streets were crowded with people having a good time. Somebody bumped into Roxie and spilled beer on her. She started to growl, but stopped herself in time.

"Well, at least no one notices us with crowds like this," said Wobar. "But I sure would like to find a place to stay. I'm exhausted."

Finally, they found a likely hotel. Wobar got a room, and moments later, Roxie climbed up the fire escape and joined him. They ate the last of their food, and Wobar got out his notebook.

"After we find the silver pipe, I'll pay everybody back, " Wobar told Roxie, "so I'm writing down Acme Air Freight and Gulf Airways. They need to be paid for getting us to New Orleans. If I get a paper route in Woodstown, eventually I'll make enough money." He sighed. His notebook was full of debts, and he knew that lots of people were mad at him.

The next morning, Wobar and Roxie slept later than usual. Roxie was already painted, and Wobar put on her leash before they went outside to explore the town. Wobar didn't have any real good ideas about how they would begin to find the magic pipe.

"I suppose we could look for it in a museum," he suggested to Roxie. "After all, it's old and valuable."

"Or we could look in the phone book," said Roxie. "Maybe Bad Bert's great-great-great-great-great-grandchildren have it."

But the phone book didn't help. Nobody was listed under Blandish. So they began walking the streets of New Orleans, hoping they would find a museum or get an idea. Finally, Wobar stopped.

"Do you see that, Roxie?" Wobar asked.

"Yes, but don't forget that I can't read. It's a sign. What does it say?"

"Madame Gazonga. Fortunes Told. Palms Read," read Wobar. He stared at the sign, which showed a gypsy reading a crystal ball. "Let's go in. If she can tell fortunes, maybe she can see what happened in the past. Maybe she can tell us where the magic pipe is."

"On the other hand," said Roxie," maybe she will see through our disguises and turn us in to the police."

"I don't think so," said Wobar. "She would see that we're only trying to do good. Anyhow, it's worth a try. We can always run if we think she's up to tricks."

Wobar went up the steps to the front door of the old house. He rang the bell. After a long wait, a little girl with long dark braids answered the door.

"Hello," said Wobar. "I'd like to have my fortune told. Is Madame Gazonga there?"

"Come in," said the girl. "She'll be with you in a moment."

Wobar and Roxie waited in a darkened room. It smelled funny, sort of smoky like a campfire, but also like flowers. Roxie was nervous.

"I don't like this place, Wobar," she said. "Let's go. There must be a better way to find the silver pipe."

Just then Madame Gazonga entered the room. She was an old woman wearing a bright flowered skirt and a purple blouse. Her hair was covered by a scarf, and she wore large gold hoops in her ears. Several long strands of pearls hung from her neck.

"Welcome, young man," she said. "I can tell that you have not come to have your fortune told. What can I do for you? I sense that you have lost something. You have come to the right place. I can see into all corners of the world."

"Well, we sort of lost something, but not really," said Wobar. "Umm, it's a bit complicated."

"Come into my parlor," said Madame Gazonga. She looked at Roxie. "I would prefer to have the animal stay here. Cats tend to put off my concentration."

"You mean Spot? She's a very good dog. No trouble at all," said Wobar.

"Young man, *nothing* escapes the eyes of Madame Gazonga. You are dressed like an old man, but you are a boy . . . with a real mustache. Very interesting. And Spot is not a dog. And you have come a long way with a problem. For ten dollars, I will help you. Do not be afraid. I will never tell your secrets, even though I can see them."

Wobar hesitated. He was convinced that Madame Gazonga could help him if anybody could. But he was worried. What if she learned about the magic pipe from him, then took it herself? What if she figured out who he was? He looked to Roxie. She nodded her head, yes. Reassured, he reached for his wallet. He would take the chance.

"Okay," he said. "Wait here, Spot. I'll be back." He paid the ten dollars and followed the fortune-teller through a doorway draped in black velvet and into her parlor.

CHAPTER 31

The Crystal Ball

∽

WOBAR SAT FACING Madame Gazonga at a round wooden table in her parlor. A crystal ball sat in the middle of the table, glowing slightly. The legs of the table were carved to look like rattlesnakes, with their mouths open and fangs exposed. Wobar shuddered. The room was nearly dark, lit only by a few candles.

"Put your fingers on the ball," she said. She put her hands on the ball, and it began to glow more brightly. "Do not tell me anything. The crystal ball will help me see all and know all."

Wobar waited. He could see vague shapes and colors moving inside the crystal ball. The fortune-teller stared intently into it. Wobar kept waiting. It seemed like ages before she spoke again.

"You have come a long way, Wobar," she said softly.

Wobar jumped. How could she know his name? That crystal ball was no fake, that was for sure.

"Do not be afraid, Wobar. I will help you. I have seen Simon the ghost. I understand why you are here. It will not be easy to find the silver pipe, but I know I can find it. More than two hundred years have passed since the pipe was stolen. This may take time. I must concentrate . . . concentrate . . . concentrate . . ."

Madame Gazonga closed her eyes. She let her head tip forward until her forehead touched the crystal ball. She gripped the ball on each side and moved her fingers over the surface. She sat up, opened her eyes, and focused again on the crystal ball.

"Bert Blandish . . . Bad Bert . . . yes, he came here to New Orleans with the magic pipe," said Madame Gazonga. "I see him clearly now . . . come in to my crystal ball, magic pipe . . . come in."

Wobar waited anxiously. He watched the fortune-teller. He tried to see the shapes moving inside the crystal ball, but it was blurry to him.

"I see a card game . . . Bad Bert is doing badly . . . There is an argument . . . A gun is pulled . . . Shots are fired . . . The silver pipe! I see the pipe! . . . Someone takes it from Bad Bert's pocket . . . another shot . . . Men are running . . ."

Silence. Wobar crossed his fingers and hoped. "Please," he thought, "please see what happens next." There was a long silence. Madame Gazonga almost appeared to be asleep. It seemed like forever before she spoke again.

"The pipe is sold . . . Years pass . . . It is sold again . . . Come to me, magic pipe. Where are you now? . . ." She looked at Wobar and shrugged. "We must have patience. The magic pipe is hidden somewhere hard for me to see. Maybe it does not want me to find it. Or maybe it is underwater or buried. My powers work best above ground."

"But isn't there something else you can do? I must find the pipe."

"Come back tonight at midnight. The bewitching hour. My crystal ball will have more strength then. The calumet will show itself. This afternoon I will send out a dove to fly over the bayous. If the pipe is buried or under water, my dove will help me. Sometimes I can almost see though her eyes."

Wobar stood up to leave. Madame Gazonga stopped him. "Take back your money, Wobar," she said. "Your heart is good. You want to help all people. I cannot take money for this. And do not worry, tonight I will succeed." She held out his ten-dollar bill.

Wobar hesitated. He really should pay her, he thought. But she refused his offer twice, so he thanked Madame Gazonga and took back his money. He promised to return at midnight, then he and Roxie left.

"What happened, Wobar?" Roxie asked as soon as they got outside.

"She was amazing! She knew my name. She said she had seen Simon in her crystal ball, and she agreed to help us find the pipe. Apparently, Bad Bert lost it in a card game, and it has been sold several times since then. But she couldn't see where it is now. We are to come back at midnight, and she will try again."

"What if this is a trap?" asked Roxie. "Maybe she read about you in the newspaper. That could be how she knew your name. You're the only boy anywhere with a mustache. Maybe if we come back tonight, the police will be waiting for us. Or maybe she *did* see the pipe in her crystal ball and is going to get it for herself this afternoon. And remember, she doesn't like cats. I could tell. That's not a good sign. Do you really think we should come back?

Wobar was troubled by what Roxie said. She could be right. But he couldn't see what else they could do.

"We have to take a chance," said Wobar. "And besides, how could she have known about Simon and Bad Bert? I'm sure she wants to help us. She even gave back my money."

Wobar sounded very sure of himself, but inside he was worried. Maybe the gypsy really would steal the pipe for herself, but he hoped not. They would soon find out. At midnight, they would know.

CHAPTER 32

X Marks the Spot

W OBAR AND ROXIE spent the rest of the day wandering around New Orleans. They sat outside the Cafe du Monde and ate sugar-covered beignets, still hot from the fryer. They stood on top of the levee by the Mississippi River and watched a man with a tuba playing jazz and blues all by himself. The music was sad, and it made Wobar feel sorry for the man, so he put a dollar bill in his music case. But time passed slowly for Wobar, and he couldn't help but worry about their midnight meeting.

For dinner, Wobar bought fish and chips, plenty for both of them, and they ate it in their hotel room. A storm blew into New Orleans, and the rain beat against the window. The wind howled. At eleven-thirty, they left the room and set off to see Madame Gazonga. By the time they arrived, they were both soaking wet. Wobar was cold and nervous. Roxie shivered.

Wobar rang the bell. A bolt of lightning struck nearby, and the thunder nearly deafened him. He waited, then rang the bell again. Still nothing. Had he misunderstood when they were to return? He counted to a hundred and rang the bell a third time, then rapped on the door with his knuckles. Finally, the door opened.

"Come in, Wobar. The time is right." Madame Gazonga led them inside and motioned for Roxie to stay in the outer room. Roxie looked upset. Wobar bent down and gave her a hug, then followed Madame Gazonga into her parlor. Lightning flashed again, filling the room with light, and then suddenly the room went dark. The lights had been knocked out by the storm. Madame Gazonga lit a candle. Wobar waited quietly as the crystal ball began to glow.

"Crystal ball of ages old, crystal ball of my mother's fold, crystal ball who knows all, now is the hour of your strength. Reach out, oh crystal ball, find for me the pipe of silver old." The room began to brighten. A bluish light came from the ball and flitted around the room. Madame Gazonga frowned and peered intently into the ball.

"Wobar, you must help me," she said. "Clear your mind of all thoughts. Think only of the magic pipe. And never move your eyes from the crystal ball. Don't look at me. No matter what happens."

Wobar was just plain scared. What did she mean no matter what happens? But he did what he was told. Images in the crystal ball suddenly came into focus. He saw the magic pipe! Madame Gazonga let out a moan and closed her eyes. Her eyelids began to flutter.

"Magic pipe, do not resist me. I must find you. By the power of ancient Saul, I command you. SHOW YOURSELF!" Sparks began to leap from the crystal ball. Wobar's hair stood on end. Just then, a clock struck twelve.

"I see water . . . a swamp . . . The pipe is being buried . . . I see a map . . . Zut! I can't read the map . . . It's too fuzzy, my eyes are too weak . . ."

Wobar sat on the edge of his chair. He scarcely dared to breathe. He stared at the crystal ball. Slowly, he saw a map coming into focus in front of him.

"Concentrate, Wobar. Study the map. My poor old eyes are too weak to read it. Hurry. The image won't last long."

Wobar studied the map. He tried his best to memorize all the details. The lights in the crystal ball began to quiver. Then the room was dark again. Only the light of the candles lit the room. The ball went dark.

"Do you have it, Wobar? Can you draw the map?"

"I saw it, but I couldn't understand it very well. There was a swamp and a place where three streams meet. There was an X marked by a large oak tree, near a freshwater spring. But there were no names on the streams. It could have been anywhere. I can draw it, but it could be anywhere."

"Three streams," said Madame Gazonga. "That's our best clue. There is only one place near New Orleans where three streams meet. It's near a place they call Teche Baudaire. My daddy used to take us fishing there. I remember a huge oak tree, too. But it was blown down in the hurricane of 1938. But with luck, maybe we can find the stump. We must go there tonight before you forget anything. I sense the time is right. The pipe will be in your hands before dawn."

Wobar was tired and wet. The storm was still raging outside, and neither he nor Roxie liked lightning. But Madame Gazonga was right. They had to search for the magic pipe before he forgot the details of the map.

"I'm ready," Wobar said. "Let's go."

CHAPTER 33

To the Swamp

W OBAR AND ROXIE climbed into Madame Gazonga's decrepit old car. She had a hard time starting it, but finally the engine caught, and they headed out of town. Rain beat against the windshield, and it was hard to see much of anything. The wipers didn't work very well. After a while, they turned onto a muddy road, which led into a vast swamp. There were no lights to be seen. They had reached the bayou.

"It's been many years since I was last here," said Madame Gazonga. "I hope I can find my way." She slowed the car as they passed a side road. "I don't think it's that one. That must be a new road, I don't remember it."

For an hour or more, they drove in silence down little dirt roads that crisscrossed the swamp. Several times they came to dead ends and had to turn around. Once they got stuck in the mud, and Wobar had to get out and push. From time to time, Wobar saw the eyes of alligators shining in the swamp as they drove by. Suddenly, Madame Gazonga pulled the car over to the side of the road and stopped.

"This is it. From here on, you will have to go by foot. If my memory serves me well, you'll find the three streams over there."

She pointed off to the right. "But you will have to find the place yourself. I'm too old to go wandering around in a swamp at night. Besides, I'm afraid of the snakes and alligators that live out there. I'll wait here for you to return." With that, she tipped back the car seat and closed her eyes.

Wobar wasn't exactly fond of snakes or alligators either. But if they wanted to find the magic pipe, he had no choice. Reluctantly, he and Roxie got out of the car.

"Look for a stump of the old tree just this side of the place where the three streams meet," called out Madame Gazonga. "That's where I remember the big oak."

Roxie lead the way through the tall grass. It was very dark, and the rain had not let up at all. Wobar's shoes squished in the soft mud as he walked along. He wished he were home in a dry bed. He hoped he wouldn't meet any alligators or poisonous snakes. He thought about turning back and waiting until daylight. But Roxie kept going and didn't seem afraid, so he followed her. Wobar tried to keep a picture of the map fresh in his mind. Suddenly, Roxie stopped.

"Wobar, there's a stream off to our left. But I smell something fishy, it's probably an alligator. What should we do?"

"Yikes!" thought Wobar. He was so nervous his mustache lost its curl. He started to sweat. He had never seen a live alligator, but everything he had ever read about them was unfavorable. An alligator could eat him in a few minutes, or drag him down to its underwater cave to eat later. He wasn't sure how well they could hear, or how fast they could move. And he didn't want to find out.

"Let's get away from here and fast! Go off toward the right,"

Wobar said. "Quietly. Maybe we can sneak by without being heard or seen. We'll have to avoid the stream for a while."

Roxie veered to her right, moving slowly and taking great care to make no sound. Wobar tried to keep his feet from making squishing sounds in the mud, but each step made a noise. Before long, they came to another stream.

"Let's follow this one downstream. Hopefully, it will meet the two others," said Wobar. "I think we're almost there."

It began to rain even harder. Even with his special ability to see in the dark, it was almost impossible for Wobar to see where he was going. Tall grasses kept slapping him in the face. Then he tripped on something and fell. He lay quietly for a minute, all covered with mud, and then suddenly he got very happy.

"Roxie! Roxie!" he said as loudly as he dared. "Come back. I think I've found it. I just tripped on a stump. This should be the stump of the old oak tree that was on the map. Please go see if the streams meet nearby. I'll wait here."

Sure enough, Roxie came back and reported that the three streams came together just ahead. Wobar tried to picture the map. Ten paces from the tree toward the largest stream. Then three paces upstream. Then an X marked the spot near a freshwater spring. That would be, he hoped, where the pipe was buried.

Slowly, Wobar paced off the distance. Since his legs weren't as long as a man's, he stretched to take long strides. He stopped when he reached the spot where he thought the pipe should be. Water was bubbling out of a small spring nearby.

"This is it, Roxie! I think we've found the place."

CHAPTER 34

Perseverance Pays Off!

◦⃝◦

IN THEIR HURRY to begin the search for the magic pipe, they had forgotten to bring a shovel. But the earth was soft and muddy, and Roxie began digging with her strong forepaws. Wobar stood by waiting as Roxie dug deeper and deeper. Within an hour, the hole was about four feet wide and more than three feet deep.

"Wobar, I can't dig much deeper. This hole is filling up with water, and the mud from the sides keeps falling in as fast as I dig it out."

"I'll help," said Wobar. He took off his shoes, rolled up his pant legs, and stepped into the hole. The hole was knee-deep in water. Roxie jumped out, splashing him.

Wobar used both hands, cupping them to scoop out the water and loose mud. The mud was gooey, and he couldn't throw it far from the hole. And as Roxie said, the sides kept falling in. The hole got wider, but didn't seem to get much deeper. Wobar worked hard, which kept him from getting cold. But after some time, Wobar started to get discouraged. What if he had remembered the map wrong? They could spend days digging holes in the mud for nothing.

"Come on, Wobar," said Roxie. "Let's get out of here. We need buckets and a shovel. This is dangerous, too. You could get trapped in the mud. It's almost like quicksand."

Roxie was right. Wobar's head was nearly at ground level now. He could be buried alive. He started to climb out, but as he did, the side of the hole caved in. He fell backward and was buried in thick, sticky mud. Just his head was sticking up. He didn't stop to wonder if he would get out alive. He just started struggling to get up, but without any luck.

Roxie lay down on the ground beside the hole and reached down a paw. Finally, Wobar pulled one arm free from the mud and grabbed her paw. With Roxie pulling, Wobar managed to stand up. But he was still waist deep in mud. He shifted his weight and felt something hard with his foot.

"Roxie! I just felt something with my foot. I think it's the pipe!"

Wobar tried to feel for the pipe with his toes, but it slipped away. It was gone, and he was still trapped in the mud. He wasn't sure, but he sensed that he was sinking deeper the longer he stood there.

"Maybe you'd better go for help, Roxie. I don't think I can get out."

"But how can I? You're the only human who can understand the language of cougars, "she said. "I'll have to dig you out myself."

Carefully, Roxie climbed down into the hole. If she got stuck or buried, they wouldn't have a chance to get out alive.

For another hour, they worked at trying to get Wobar free. Wobar scooped out mud and water. Roxie dug with her paws, moving mud away from Wobar and toward the other side of the hole. Finally, Wobar was able to move his feet, even though he was still knee-deep in mud.

Unless the side caves in again, we'll be all right now," said Wobar. "I'll move around trying to feel for the pipe with my toes."

"Be careful, Wobar," urged Roxie. "You were nearly buried alive the first time. We should go back and get help. The sides could collapse again any minute." She crawled out of the hole.

Wobar was determined to find the pipe, and he was pretty sure it was in the loose mud at the bottom of the hole. He believed that perseverance always pays off. There was no one he could ask for help. Squish, squish. He moved slowly through the mud, probing for the pipe with his feet.

"Roxie!" he yelled at last. "I think I've got it! I've got my foot on something here!" Wobar bent down and stuck his hand deep into the mud. He grabbed the object and slowly pulled it out of the mud. He couldn't see much, but his hands told the story. It was a pipe. It clearly felt like metal. And he felt an odd vibration coming from the pipe that tickled his fingers.

"We did it! It's the pipe!" yelled Wobar. He worked his way to the side of the hole. "Give me a paw and help me up."

Roxie helped Wobar up. Just as he got out, the side caved in all at once. Wobar breathed a sigh of relief. He had just escaped.

"We've got it! We've got it! We've found the magic pipe!" Wobar could have jumped with joy, but he was too tired.

The sun was just coming up, and the rain had stopped as Wobar and Roxie reached the car. Madame Gazonga was still there, sound asleep. They woke her up.

"We got it! We found the magic pipe!" That's all Wobar could say. He fell asleep, repeating it over and over, as they drove toward town.

CHAPTER 35

Mr. Longsworth's Hotel

WHEN WOBAR GOT back to the hotel, the desk clerk gave him a funny look. He was covered with mud and even had a muddy mustache. But the clerk didn't say anything. New Orleans is full of people doing crazy things, and he'd probably seen worse. Wobar got to the room, opened the window, and Roxie hopped in off the fire escape.

As soon as Wobar and Roxie scrubbed up, they went right to bed. They slept for a long time. When they woke up, the sun was shining brightly in their window. It was late afternoon. Roxie yawned, showing off all her teeth.

"Well, we did it," said Roxie. "We found the magic calumet."

Wobar took the pipe out of its hiding place under the mattress. He had washed off the mud before they went to bed. It was beautiful. It had a long handle decorated with an eagle, a bear, a fox, and an otter. All the animals looked like they were friends. The bear had a kind look on its face, and the eagle carried a ribbon of some sort. None of them looked fierce or warlike.

"We've got the pipe all right," said Wobar. "But our work isn't finished yet. Don't forget that somehow we have to get it to the presi-

dent of the United States. That might not be easy. I mean, I don't think we can just walk into the White House and hand it to him. And besides, he lives in Washington, D.C. That's a long way from here."

Roxie let out a groan. She hadn't thought that far ahead. In fact, neither of them had thought about this part.

"Maybe we could phone the president and explain what we have," said Wobar, "Then he would invite us to the White House. He might even send Air Force One to pick us up."

"Do you really think he would believe our story?" asked Roxie. "Do you think *anyone* would believe that we learned about a magic pipe from a ghost named Simon? Or that Madame Gazonga used her crystal ball to help us find it? I don't think anybody is going to believe that we have a magic silver pipe that can stop wars. I believe that this pipe has powers like no other, but I'm not sure I can convince anyone else. Even if we could get the president of the United States on the phone, which I doubt, would he listen to us? He'd probably think we were crazy."

Wobar wanted to cry, but he didn't. Roxie wanted to let out a loud yowl, but knew someone might hear her, so she didn't.

They had found the pipe, but now they couldn't figure out how to give it to the president. Unless they did, Simon would always remain a ghost, and countries would get in wars every time they squabbled with their neighbors. All their efforts would have been for nothing.

"Well, let's go get something to eat," said Roxie. "I'm starved. We'll think of something. Maybe in New Orleans they serve rabbit stew. I always think better on a full stomach, anyway."

So Wobar and Roxie left the hotel and went to the marketplace near the Mississippi River. Wobar decided to try the local specialties, so he got a muffaletta sandwich for himself and a big piece of fried alligator meat for Roxie, who was waiting outside, back in her disguise as a dog.

They wandered down the street looking for a quiet place to sit down and eat. Suddenly, Wobar stopped.

"Look at that hotel, Roxie," he said.

"We don't need a hotel," snapped Roxie. "I'm hungry and want to find a place where we can eat."

"No, you don't understand," said Wobar. "That's the Longsworth Hotel. I bet it's owned by C. Clement Longsworth, the man we saved in New York. Maybe he would help us. Maybe he would believe our story."

Roxie spotted a park just down the street, so they hurried down there to eat. After worrying about alligators last night, Roxie was looking forward to eating one, instead of the other way around. She liked it. It tasted a little like fish. For a moment, she didn't worry about anything. She gobbled her meal and licked her lips.

"I think you're right, Wobar," said Roxie. "Didn't the newspaper say that Mr. Longsworth is supposed to be one of the richest men in America? I bet he knows the president."

"I bet he does, too. And since we saved him, I'm sure he would at least be willing to try to help us. He'll probably know what to do."

"It's worth a try," said Roxie. "And he won't do anything that will get us in trouble, that's for sure."

So Wobar and Roxie approached the Longsworth Hotel. Wobar tied Roxie's leash to a parking meter in front of the hotel and went in. He went right up to the front desk.

"Excuse me," he said, "is this hotel owned by Mr. C. Clement Longsworth?"

"Of course," said the man behind the desk.

"Well, I need to talk to him."

"Sorry, but Mr. Longsworth doesn't live in New Orleans. The main office is in Houston. But he's in semi-retirement, and he is very rarely in the office. What do you need him for?"

"I'm a friend," said Wobar. "Could you please give me his phone number?"

"No. I can't give you his home phone number, but I'll give you a number at the main office. But I wouldn't count on being able to get in touch with him. He travels a lot and is a very busy man."

The man wrote down a number on a piece of paper and gave it to Wobar. Wobar left the hotel feeling pretty discouraged. If he couldn't talk to Mr. Longsworth, how would they ever get the pipe to the president?

CHAPTER 36

Telling All

⟡

WOBAR AND ROXIE went back to their hotel to place the call to Houston. Wobar wasn't used to making long distance phone calls. He was a little nervous dialing the number.

"Hello, Longsworth Hotels Incorporated. How may I direct your call?"

"I'd like to speak to Mr. Longsworth," said Wobar.

"I'm sorry, but Mr. Longsworth is not available at this time. What is it that you need? Perhaps someone else can help you. Do you have a complaint or a suggestion? I can connect you with Customer Service."

"No," said Wobar. "It's personal. I'm a friend, or sort of a friend. I really need to talk to him. "

"I'm sorry, but that's impossible. If you wish to leave your name and number, perhaps he'll call you back. But you should realize that he is a very busy man. Are you sure someone else couldn't help you?"

Wobar left his name and number and hung up. He hoped Mr. Longsworth would remember his name. He hoped he would call back.

Wobar and Roxie waited for three hours, but the phone didn't ring.

"I'm hungry again," said Roxie. "Let's go get some food."

"No," said Wobar. We'd better wait here. I would hate to miss the phone call." If it ever comes, he thought.

They waited and waited, but the phone didn't ring. Finally, Wobar gave up, and they went to bed, hungry and disappointed. But Wobar couldn't sleep. He was busy trying to figure out what to do next. Suddenly, he jumped. The phone was ringing. He turned on the light and grabbed for it.

"Hello, is this Wobar? This is Mr. Longsworth."

Wobar was so excited he could barely think of what to say. "Yes, this is Wobar," he finally blurted out.

"I'd like to thank you for saving my life in New York. You are a very brave young man!" said Mr. Longsworth. "But what are you doing in New Orleans? You're a long way from home."

Wobar started from the beginning. He explained about biting his teacher and then running away from home. He told how he met Roxie and how she had been shot. He was afraid Mr. Longsworth wouldn't believe the part about Simon and the silver pipe, but he did his best to be convincing. Mr. Longsworth listened to it all, their journey from Woodstown to New Orleans, and how they finally found the magic pipe. He never interrupted Wobar once. There was a long pause at the end of Wobar's tale.

"Well, that certainly was quite an adventure. What can I do now to help you?" asked Mr. Longsworth.

"We want to give the peace pipe to the president of the United States. That's what Simon promised the Indian over two hundred years ago. Could you help us do that?" asked Wobar.

"Well, I can't promise a thing. I've met the president a few times, and I donated some money to his last election campaign. I'll see what I can do. I do believe your story about the magic pipe, but I can't promise that he will. Let's see, it's nearly midnight in Washington, so I can't call tonight. But I'll call first thing in the morning and see what I can do. In the meantime, try to get some sleep."

"Oh, thank you so much, Mr. Longsworth." said Wobar. "That would be the best reward you could ever give us."

Roxie and Wobar curled up in bed. Roxie purred quietly as she fell asleep, but Wobar was too excited to get much sleep. It was like the night before Christmas and his birthday rolled into one.

The sun was barely up when the phone rang. It was Mr. Longsworth.

"Good morning, Wobar, this is Mr. Longsworth speaking. I've got some good news for you. I spoke to the president while he was at breakfast this morning and explained about the silver pipe. He's a little skeptical about the story, but said he would do anything to achieve world peace. He can see you this afternoon at four. I told him you'd be there."

"That's terrific!" Then Wobar paused to think. Washington was a long way from New Orleans. "But how in the world will I ever get to Washington by tonight? It took us days to get here."

"Don't worry about a thing, Wobar. I'll have a driver come by to pick you up. I'll fly over from Houston in my private jet and get you. And Roxie, too. After all, without Roxie I would have died in the fire. We'll meet the president together, and you can present him with the magic pipe."

Wobar thanked Mr. Longsworth and hung up. He could barely believe his good luck! He really would be able to present the magic calumet to the president of the United States!

CHAPTER 37

The Presidential Medal

❧

FOR WOBAR AND Roxie, the hand of the clock seemed to move in slow motion. Mr. Longsworth said someone would come by to pick them up and take them to the airport at one o'clock. Wobar gave Roxie a bath. He decided it was better to be safe than sorry, so he painted her to look like a Dalmatian, even though he hoped there would be no trouble traveling with a cougar.

Wobar went out and bought all new clothes—shirt, pants, and even a new pair of shoes. He wanted to look spiffy to meet the president. Buying the new clothes used up most of the money they had left, which made him a little nervous.

They were both very hungry, so Wobar brought back a big order of fried chicken. But he gave most of his to Roxie because he was too excited to eat much. Roxie always had a good appetite, and she ate it, bones and all.

The limousine came right on time. The driver had been told that Roxie was going to ride with him, but he still looked a little bit nervous. He kept the glass closed between the front and back of the limo. When they arrived at the airport, he opened the door and

directed them toward the waiting room for passengers of private planes.

"You must be Wobar," said the man at the desk. "We've been waiting for you. Mr. Longsworth just called, and his jet will be here shortly."

Moments later, they saw a small jet taxi up to the terminal where they were waiting. It stopped, and Mr. Longsworth got out and came inside.

"Good afternoon, Wobar," he said. "I'm so glad to meet you. And that must be your friend Roxie, the cougar. She's a fine-looking animal. But why is she painted like that?" Roxie sat and put out her paw to shake hands with Mr. Longsworth.

"That's her disguise, Mr. Longsworth. She's supposed to look like a firedog, you know, a Dalmatian. It's so no one will think I'm traveling with a wild animal. People tend to get nervous when they see a cougar. We do it to keep out of trouble."

Mr. Longsworth smiled. "I dare say you've had your share of trouble, disguise or no," said Mr. Longsworth. "But all that's over. From here on, I'll take care of everything. Let's go. My plane is waiting."

They left the terminal and got on the plane. The flight attendant explained that everyone had to wear a seat belt, even cougars. So Roxie sat up in the seat, and Wobar attached her seat belt.

The flight to Washington was uneventful. It was a smooth ride, and Roxie didn't get sick. A big black limousine was waiting for them when they arrived. The president had sent it from the White House. They were a little early, and Roxie had a request for Wobar.

"Do you think we could go to our hotel first, before we meet the president? I feel silly all painted to look like a dog. I'm a cougar and proud of it. If I'm going to meet the president, I want to look like a cougar."

Wobar explained the situation to Mr. Longsworth, who told the driver to go by the Longsworth Hotel. For once, Roxie didn't have to sneak up the fire escape. They were expected at the hotel, and a suite was ready for them. Wobar gave Roxie a quick bath, dried her off, and they were ready to meet the president. Roxie looked at herself in the mirror and quickly groomed her whiskers. She knew she was a very handsome animal.

Their limousine arrived at the White House right on time. They were ushered inside and took a seat outside the Oval Office. The security people kept staring at Roxie, and Wobar overheard them discussing whether a wild animal of that size should be allowed to get near the president. Wobar's exceptional hearing allowed him to hear the guards talking about his mustache, too, wondering if he was really just a boy. Just then the president opened the door to the Oval Office.

"Why it's my old friend, C. Clement Longsworth. Good to see you again, Clem," said the president. "And this must be Wobar . . . and Roxie. I've heard a lot about you both. Please do come in." They all went into the Oval Office. "I've invited the press to send a few of their people. After all, this is a very special day."

As soon as the television crews were ready, the president asked Wobar to tell about the magic pipe. Wobar explained about the Indian who had tried to bring the silver pipe to General George Washington, and what the pipe could do, and how it had been stolen. He sort of skipped over the part about Simon, since lots of people don't believe in ghosts. He unwrapped the pipe, taking it out of the towel he had used to protect it while traveling, and presented it to the president.

"Wobar," said the president, "on behalf of the people and government of the United States of America, I would like to thank you. I will try to use this pipe to help to spread peace throughout the world. I hope that we can stop the wars in progress and help all people to get along. As a token of my appreciation, I would like to present you with this Presidential Medal of Honor." He got up and pinned a gold medal on Wobar. "And," he said, "for the first time in the history of America, I have a Medal of Honor for an animal, Roxie. She helped you find the pipe, so she deserves a medal, too."

Fortunately, the president had thought to have the medal put on a long loop of ribbon since he couldn't pin it on Roxie. He slipped it over her head.

Roxie didn't smile, even though she wanted to. She knew her teeth were ferocious looking when she smiled, and the security people still looked nervous.

"Congratulations and my thanks to you both," said the president.

After they posed for pictures with the president, Roxie and Wobar left. They had finally done it. Their job was done. Now they could return to Woodstown. Wobar knew his parents would see them on the six o'clock news. He hoped that all would be forgiven.

CHAPTER 38

Paying Off Debts

T HAT NIGHT, WOBAR, Roxie, and Mr. Longsworth had dinner in the fine dining room of the Longsworth Hotel. As a special treat for Roxie, Mr. Longsworth had arranged to have roast rabbit for her. He and Wobar had huge steaks. Several people came up to Wobar to thank him for what he had done. A few even asked for autographs. No one teased him about his mustache. Everybody had seen them on TV or on the front page of the newspaper. Wobar and Roxie were famous.

"Well, Wobar," said Mr. Longsworth, "you've done a wonderful thing. Tomorrow, my jet will fly you back to Woodstown. I'll come along because I want to meet your parents. How do you feel?"

"Gee, it feels great. I'm really looking forward to seeing my family. I just have a few little things worrying me."

"Tell me what's on your mind, Wobar, and perhaps I can help."

"Well, first, I hope that my teacher and the principal of my school aren't still mad at me. I've really worried about being sent off to reform school," said Wobar.

"You don't have to worry about that, "said Mr. Longsworth. "I called the principal of your school just after the six o'clock news. He

said he was proud to have you as a student in his school. And Mrs. Murphy said she'd help you make up the work you missed while you were away."

"Wow, that's terrific!" said Wobar. He took another bite of the big banana split in front of him. "Um . . . another thing has to do with Roxie. I know she needs to live in the woods up on Grantham Mountain, but I hope my parents will let her come in the house and visit from time to time. Maybe sleep on my bed once in a while. We've gotten to be real good friends." Roxie gazed at Mr. Longsworth very seriously.

"Naturally, I wondered about that, too," said Mr. Longsworth. "I had to call them to let them know what time you'd be arriving tomorrow. I took the liberty of discussing that with them."

"What did they say?" Wobar asked. Roxie let out a series of chuffs. Mr. Longsworth couldn't understand Roxie, but he got the idea. They were both really anxious to know the answer.

"Well, quite frankly, they didn't think it was a very good idea. Roxie belongs in the wild, they said. And you have a cat and a dog. They were worried that Roxie might attack them. Or vice versa. She is a wild animal, you know."

Wobar groaned. Roxie's eyes looked very sad.

"But I told them how well behaved Roxie is and reminded them that Roxie saved my life and won the Presidential Medal of Honor. Finally, they agreed to let her visit any time she wants."

"Yahoo!" shouted Wobar. Roxie clapped her front paws the way she'd seen people do. Her paws didn't make any noise, but Mr. Longsworth understood.

"Is there anything else worrying you, Wobar? Since you saved my life, I'd be glad to do anything I could to help you." Wobar looked at Roxie. "Well, it's not for me, really, it's for Roxie. She heard that one of her children is in a zoo in the next state. Do you suppose you might be able to arrange to have him brought back to Grantham Mountain and set free?" Roxie was all ears, waiting.

"I should be able to arrange that. In exchange for a generous donation to their zoo, I suppose they would be willing to let him go. Roxie is known all over the country now, and that should help."

Roxie turned to Wobar and said, "That's wonderful. Please tell Mr. Longsworth how much I appreciate that. I've been worrying about my son ever since I saw those lions in the Central Park Zoo. And thank you for thinking of him, Wobar." Wobar translated what Roxie said for Mr. Longsworth.

"Is there anything else, Wobar? Don't hesitate to ask."

"Well, Mr. Longsworth, there is one last thing," admitted Wobar. "I owe some people money. It's going to take years to pay it all back, even if I get a paper route and save all my allowance, too. But that's okay, I should pay them back myself."

"I would be delighted to help you pay them," said Mr. Longsworth. "After all, I promised you a reward for saving me. I would like to consider you like one of my grandchildren and help you any way I can. Who do you owe?"

Wobar got out his notebook. "Well, I owe the veterinarian for saving Roxie. Then there were some groceries I took from Spencer's Family Market. I kept a list so I could pay them back. And there's the boat in St. Louis that I borrowed. I should pay for the repairs of the bullet holes." Wobar paused to think. "Then there's Acme Air Freight and Gulf Airways. We tricked them into flying us to New Orleans. I need to pay them back."

"Why those few things won't add up to much. The reward I

planned to give you will easily cover that with plenty left over," said Mr. Longsworth.

"Really? Wow, that's neat! Then I can send a present to Madame Gazonga for helping me. And next summer when Oscar the hobo comes to visit his sister, I can give him something nice, too."

Wobar and Roxie were very happy. They were also very tired after their long day, so they thanked Mr. Longsworth and headed off to bed. Tomorrow they would be home.

CHAPTER 39

Going Home

⚬⚬

THE NEXT MORNING, Wobar ate a big breakfast of waffles with real maple syrup, and Roxie wolfed down a heaping plate of sausages. Then Mr. Longsworth came by, and they all got into a limousine and went to the airport. His jet plane was ready for them, and minutes later they were airborne, heading home.

When they were nearing the airport close to Woodstown, Wobar saw Grantham Mountain. He pointed it out to Roxie and Mr. Longsworth, who asked the pilot to fly close by it. Roxie got very excited.

"Look, Wobar," she said. That's my old cave. And my favorite hunting ground for rabbits. Say, we never did eat any rabbit ice cream, did we?"

Wobar laughed. It would be good to be back. Roxie would soon be able to go hunting again, and he would be with his family. And Roxie could come to visit. Mr. Longsworth had already helped them solve so many problems.

Wobar's parents and his brothers and sisters were all waiting for him at the airport. The mayor of Woodstown was there, and Mr. Benson, the principal of the school. Wobar hugged everybody in his family and shook hands with the mayor and Mr. Benson. Roxie was

wearing her medal and looked very proud. She sat up and put out a paw so people could shake with her, too. Somebody took pictures for the local newspaper, the *Woodstown Valley News*.

Wobar, Roxie, and Mr. Longsworth rode into Woodstown with the mayor. He had an old convertible, and they rode with the top down, even though it was kind of cold.

When they got to Woodstown, everybody in town lined the streets, waiting for them. Mr. Benson had let all the children out of school to greet Wobar. They were there, waving. The mayor drove slowly up Main Street. Roxie and Wobar waved to everybody, and the crowds cheered. Some people held up signs saying "Welcome Home Wobar" and "Thanks for Finding the Peace Pipe." The mayor turned the car around, and they rode down Main Street again, waving. Wobar's mustache tickled his nose as it blew in the wind.

The mayor stopped the car in front of the Town Hall and made a speech. He thanked Wobar, Roxie, Mr. Longsworth, the president, and even some people Wobar had never heard of. He talked too long, but finally someone started singing "For He's a Jolly Good Fellow" about Wobar, and the mayor stopped talking, and they all went home.

Wobar's mother invited Mr. Longsworth to stay for dinner and even spend the night.

"Thanks very much, but my jet is waiting to take me back to Houston. You have a very brave son. Here is a check as his reward for saving my life. I will always consider Wobar one of my grandchildren." Then he shook hands with everyone, thanked Wobar again, and left.

After Wobar told his family all his adventures, he took Roxie upstairs to show her his room. "You know, Roxie," he said, once they were alone, "there is still one thing left for us to do."

"What's that, Wobar?"

"We have to go back to the haunted house. I want to see if Simon the ghost has gone off to heaven now that we've found the magic pipe and given it to the president."

So after supper, Wobar and Roxie slipped away and headed for the haunted house. Although Wobar would have liked to see Simon one last time, he hoped that Simon had gone to heaven.

When they arrived at the haunted house, Wobar took a deep breath. "Well, now we find out if Simon was right," he said to Roxie. They went inside. "Hello? Anybody home?"

They heard a familiar rattling of chains in the basement, then a crash. "Simon is that you? This is Wobar! We found the pipe! We gave it to the president!" The cellar door opened, and Simon appeared.

"Simon, what happened? We thought you'd be gone! But you're still a ghost."

Wobar was terribly disappointed. It was wonderful that the magic pipe would be used to stop wars. But what about Simon? Was he stuck as a ghost forever?

"Welcome back, Wobar and Roxie," said Simon. "Yes, I'm still a ghost. There is still one thing that has to be done."

"Oh no!" said Wobar. "I thought our adventures were over." Wobar couldn't believe it. They had gone all the way to New Orleans to find the pipe. They had been shot at, chased, and nearly buried alive. They had gotten the pipe and given it to the president. What else was there to do? Had he forgotten something Simon told him?

"Don't worry, Wobar," said Simon. "The last thing is very easy. It's for me to do. Here goes! Thank you very much, Wobar. Thank you, Roxie!" And then with a wink and a smile, Simon disappeared.

Postscript

A WEEK AFTER THE president received the magic calumet, dawn came quietly on a battlefield in a faraway land. An old man walked to the edge of a wide river and began to sing. His voice carried well in the still of the morning. The strong sun bathed all in its light. Across the river, one man laid down his rifle, then another. Then three put down their guns on the old man's side of the river. The magic had begun.

A note on illustrating (and reading) Wobar

Joshua Yunger

READING IS A skill just like any other. Some are born to read, and others, like me, have a hard road to travel on the way to achieving this ever-important skill. As a learning disabled, dyslexic third-grader, I struggled with word comprehension and often gave up after the fifth time through a difficult paragraph. My best bet for a good printed story was a comic book. They served me well. The visuals would always pull me through.

Word books, as I called them, were very intimidating indeed. That is until my stepdad, Henry, handed me his typed manuscript for his book *Wobar*. He wanted my thoughts as a young reader of the story he had told one summer while he was in college and finally written as a book.

I was worried. But I started in. To my great surprise, I was reading as fast as I ever had! On top of that, I was getting every little detail. This was the first time a book had read me. The first time a book had dragged me through it as if it were pulling me by a rope tied to my brain. The way it was written, with its short, cliff-hanging chapters, was just what I needed to get me into that next skill level. I read it in one long night under the covers with a flashlight. It was magic for me.

Some twenty-five years later, I have now illustrated *Wobar*. I did my first drawing of *Wobar* when I was ten, and I realize now that Henry and I have been working on it, off and on, the whole time. I love thinking of Henry's faith in me as an artist even way back then, and he will always be the author who made me realize I could really read.

Acknowledgments

I LEARNED THE ART of storytelling from my grandfather, Henry Homeyer Sr. (1878–1953), who encouraged my sister, Ruth Anne, and me to sneak away to his basement den during nap time to listen to his wonderful original tales.

My parents, Henry Jr. and Elfrieda Homeyer, helped me to develop a love for books, particularly those with a good story. They read aloud to me many of the classic tales, and when I became a good reader, introduced me to the wonderful books of Thornton W. Burgess and Walter R. Brooks. The *Freddy the Pig* books by Brooks made me want to believe that animals can talk and think as we do. Then Tom Sawyer and Huck Finn made me want to run away on a big adventure—which I did as an adult when I went to Africa. *Wobar* is a thank-you to them.

The children of Saxtons River, Vermont, were my first guinea pigs, listening all gathered in that wonderful circle under a big maple tree as I told the tale of *Wobar*, episode by episode, during the summer of 1966, when I had the pleasure of running the town recreation program as a summer job. Some of those first *Wobar* fans were John and Bobby Hitchcock, Ruth Fry, Frannie Rogenski, Steve Saunders, Susie Frazer, Charlie Hancock, Ellie Choukas, Keith and Tom Lockerby, Michael, Debby, and Richard Sprague, Richie Rice, Debra Johnson, Grace Boyd, Carolyn Gibson, Debbie Fletcher, Billy Turner, Peter Higgins, Peggy Sue Gibson, Scott Carroll, Judy Griffin, Dayle Knight, Tim Hemingway, Paula Page, Vicki Atwood, and my coworker Tony Dambrava. My thanks to all the parents who heard *Wobar* secondhand, and encouraged me to write it as a book. My thanks to Barbara Skapa and John Gruwell in Dakar, Senegal, who took care of me while I labored over the book.

Thanks to Kurn Hattin Homes for feeding and lodging Tony and me that summer and especially to Gwen Hitchcock who was our surrogate mother.

By the time I got back to America in the summer of 1982, after ten years living abroad, I had a finished draft, and I shared it with other young readers, including Lisa and Becky Lasor of Athens, Ohio, and my sister Ruth Anne's daughter, Sarah Mitchell. But my most enthusiastic fan was my stepson, Josh Yunger, who has illustrated this book almost thirty years after he first read it.

That same year, I knocked on the door of Caldecott Award–winning illustrator Trina Schart Hyman of Lyme, New Hampshire, to see if she would do the drawings. She offered me great encouragement and stayed up late to read the manuscript all in one night, but she said she couldn't illustrate it. She wrote two of her publishers on my behalf, but *Wobar*'s time hadn't yet come.

After *Wobar* languished in a drawer for years, I picked it up again in the late 1990s. David Gee of Cornish, New Hampshire, was kind enough to scan it to a computer disc for me, page by page, to make revisions and editing easier.

Then Nardi Reeder Campion, my mentor and friend, convinced me that *Wobar* had to be published and helped me to edit and rewrite it. Without her enthusiasm, *Wobar* never would have made it to press.

My thanks to Willa and Gavin McGough of Plainfield, New Hampshire, who read *Wobar* in its final version and suggested that I should give each chapter a title. My partner Cindy Heath offered advice and encouragement as *Wobar* neared completion.

Finally, I must thank my publishers Carole and Ib Bellew who not only published *Wobar* but whose suggestions strengthened the book and whose keen eyes ensured consistency and accuracy throughout.